"How did you know I was Am

"Your accent. I've done some business there, in California."

"California is beautiful."

"But you're not from there."

She met his gaze, and a tiny grin touched the corners of her mouth. "No." He watched her lips as she sipped her wine.

Destin waited for her to say more after she put down her glass, but he waited in vain. My, she was reserved. *Maybe she's married*, he immediately thought, but her pink-tipped fingers were bare of jewelry. Could she be traveling alone? He'd heard of American women coming to Brazil for plastic surgery, but he couldn't possibly see where she would need any.

"Maybe I should guess?" She only glanced at him. "You're from New York, it's your first time in Brazil, and you're here on a spa vacation."

She smirked and turned to him. "Yes. Yes. And no."

"No vacation? You're here on business? That's too bad," he said after she gave a brief nod. "Brazil is the perfect place for pleasure."

Her brows rose. "Is that why you're here? Pleasure?"

He w   ft as it
look

Dear Reader,

Have you ever wanted someone in spite of your better judgment? Felt the intense rush of desire for someone you shouldn't? Yeah, me, too. And that's what happened to Nicole Parks when she met Destin Dechamps. Both are after the same vineyard in the lush region of Brazil's Rio Grande do Sul, and neither is giving it up.

Still holding on to past tragedy, Destin isn't looking for love, yet he can't deny his attraction to the beautiful stranger who flew across the world and landed on his doorstep. These two didn't expect to be each other's obstacle and they certainly didn't expect to fall for each other. Things get spicy when they come to a mutually beneficial arrangement. It just goes to show that sometimes love finds you when and where you least expect it.

So tell me, who was your unexpected desire? Drop by chloeblakebooks.com and let me know.

Happy reading,

Chloe Blake

A
TASTE OF
DESIRE

Chloe Blake

HARLEQUIN® KIMANI™ ROMANCE

Recycling programs
for this product may
not exist in your area.

ISBN-13: 978-1-335-21657-1

A Taste of Desire

Copyright © 2018 by Tamara Lynch

All rights reserved. The reproduction, transmission or utilization of this
work in whole or in part in any form by any electronic, mechanical or
other means, now known or hereinafter invented, including xerography,
photocopying and recording, or in any information storage or retrieval
system, is forbidden without written permission. For permission please
contact Harlequin Kimani, 225 Duncan Mill Road, Toronto, Ontario
M3B 3K9, Canada.

This is a work of fiction. Names, characters, places and incidents are
either the product of the author's imagination or are used fictitiously,
and any resemblance to actual persons, living or dead, business establishments,
events or locales is entirely coincidental.

® and TM are trademarks of Harlequin Enterprises Limited or its corporate
affiliates. Trademarks indicated with ® are registered in the United States
Patent and Trademark Office, the Canadian Intellectual Property Office and in
other countries.

For questions and comments about the quality of this book please contact us
at CustomerService@Harlequin.com.

HARLEQUIN®
™ www.Harlequin.com

Printed in U.S.A.

Chloe Blake can be found dreaming up stories while she is traveling the world or just sitting on her couch in Brooklyn, NY. When she is not writing sexy novels, she is at the newest wine bar, taking random online classes, binge-watching Netflix or searching for her next adventure. Readers can find out more about Chloe and her books from her website at www.chloeblakebooks.com.

Books by Chloe Blake

Harlequin Kimani Romance

A Taste of Desire

For the strong women in my life. Because every time you fall, you get right back up.

Acknowledgments

I am so grateful…to my readers. Seeing your comments and supportive messages always gives me joy.

To my agent, Christine Whitthohn, for your constant support and guidance.

To Shannon Criss and the editorial team for making my dream of being a Harlequin Kimani author come true.

A huge shout-out to Jane Austen, with whom I share a birthday, and had I not visited an astrologer who told me that tidbit, I may not have become a writer.

I'm lucky to have friends from all walks of life that are like family. There is no way I could ever repay the unwavering support of my writing group: Ami, Nadia, Anna and Saga, you are my soul sisters, my coven and the loves of my life. Let's never stop creating, never stop drinking wine, never stop exploring the world and never stop dreaming bigger.

And to Amy, my sister, soul mate and fellow motherless daughter, you know me better than anyone, and yet you still stick around. I love you. Thank you for always being there for me.

Chapter 1

Nicole Parks burst from the bathroom of her hotel suite and rummaged through her suitcase. Bras, panties, a flat iron and a jam-packed makeup bag landed on the king-size bed. She sat up and aggressively squirted Visine into her eyes then gulped the fresh coffee she'd made from the in-room coffeemaker. Then she dove for her other suitcase.

Her fifteen-hour flight to the Rio Grande do Sul region of Brazil had come with a pounding post-flight headache. The blazing hot thirty-minute car ride to Porto Alegre, the capital, hadn't helped. She'd virtually passed out after checking into her hotel that afternoon, but now that nap, although refreshing, was screwing with her inner clock. Good thing her client chose the restaurant in her hotel for their business dinner. She had twenty minutes to be downstairs.

Ten minutes went by, and Nicole turned to check her appearance in the floor-length mirror: black, sleeveless, form-fitting dress, mascara and nude lipstick in place, sleek black shoulder-length hair—frizzing slightly, but so far, so good—and mahogany arms and legs shimmering with lotion.

She flipped her hair over her shoulder, gesturing to her reflection. *I have a head for business and a bod for sin. Anything wrong with that?* It was her favorite quote from the movie *Working Girl*. And she definitely was a working girl, since she was the only female international real estate broker and attorney at the New York City branch of Kingsley's.

You got this. Smooth sailing. She whispered positive mantras to herself. She loved this business: selling gorgeous properties, seeing the world, making the money. Not too shabby for a little girl from Brooklyn. Closing a deal fed her soul. It was better than sex, not that she was having any.

Dressed to impress, she reached for her phone and sighed. After locating the passcode on the corner desk, she connected to the Wi-Fi and was instantly bombarded with texts, emails and voice mail messages. She itched to go through them, noting several from her boss, but they had to wait.

Clutch and phone in hand, she rushed toward the elevator in her six-inch heels. Just as she jammed the button, a call came through. Her best friend Liz's name popped up and Nicole bit her lip, knowing she shouldn't answer.

"Liz, I can't talk right now. I'm meeting a client." Nicole punched the elevator button again.

"Nicole, where the hell have you been? I've been trying you for hours." Uh-oh. Liz was clearly irritated. As a psychologist with a weekly radio show, Dr. Elizabeth Hines had heard it all, and usually nothing got through that calm exterior.

"Brazil. I got here hours ago, and I'm off to meet a client."

"South America Brazil? I thought you were in Paris?"

"Um, that was yesterday."

"This is why you don't have a man."

Nicole jerked her neck back. "Oh, really, Dr. Love? When was the last time you got roses on Valentine's Day? And if traveling is a direct correlation to being single, then what's your excuse? You haven't left the country—no wait, you haven't left New York—since you got your PhD which was…let me think… Y2K." Nicole smiled when Liz let out a loud breath.

"I didn't call you to throw shade around. Dani needs us."

Nicole sobered. "Why? What happened?"

"Remember that Tinder date she had the other night?"

"Yeah. The guy with the four cats?" Nicole rolled her eyes. She commended Dani for continuing to put herself out there on those dating apps, but she had to stop meeting up with every guy who threw her a wink.

"He sent her a two-page email saying she's everything he's looking for in a woman, except for her weight, and wondered if she was interested in transforming herself. He sent her some basic workout tips and offered to pay for a trainer."

"Oh, my God," Nicole sneered. "Who does this cat-hoarding awful man think he is? Dani is beautiful and voluptuous. What is wrong with people?"

"I don't know, but I am so over men."

"Ditto." Nicole exhaled. "No one has ever offered to pay for my trainer."

There had been a few significant men in Nicole's life, but none had stuck it out for the long haul. Her last relationship ended when her ex suggested that no man wanted a woman who worked as much as she did. Yet he hadn't been spouting that nonsense when she had treated him to a couples spa weekend in Indonesia for his birthday. *Jerk.*

Sure, she used to want the fairy tale—man, dog, kids—but the more she unsuccessfully dated and the older she got, the farther away that dream started to float. It was time for a new plan.

"Liz, please tell me she isn't devastated."

"No, just feeling hopeless. I called because I wanted us to take her out, get her mind off of it. What are you doing in Brazil?"

"Getting ready to sell a burnt-down winery to the highest American bidder. The owner is only in his thirties, but we're talking serious old money."

"Mmm. Is he single?"

"He's French, so it probably doesn't matter. Regardless, I don't date clients. From his dossier he sounds like a trust-fund baby who is no doubt bristling at the fact that I'm a woman."

"Wait till he sees you negotiate."

"Damn right." Nicole watched her floor number light up. "Okay, I gotta go."

"Wait! What happened at the adoption agency?"

Nicole groaned. "They denied me."

"I was afraid of that, Nicole."

"I know, Liz. You've made your position clear. Could you slip out of shrink mode for one second and be the supportive friend that I've known for eight years?"

The elevator doors opened, and Nicole was relieved that it was empty. She held it for a brief second as Liz continued.

"Look, you know I think you deserve to have a child, but your lifestyle is not attractive to adoption agencies or parents choosing adoptive parents."

"Well, that's what they said."

"What else did they say?"

"That a nanny was not a full-time parent."

Liz chuckled. "Did you give them the au pair speech?"

"Don't laugh. They were not impressed. But, honestly, what better way for a kid to learn a second language?"

"Nicole, if you've really decided to go this route, maybe you should think about insemination."

"Oh, God, I cannot get pregnant."

"Why? You're only thirty-five. Women are having babies in their fifties these days."

"I travel too much."

"See—you don't know what you want."

"Yes, I do!" Afraid they'd get cut off if she stepped in, Nicole slapped her hand against the closing elevator door, pushing it open. "I want a kid and I'm done waiting around for Prince Charming, because he doesn't exist!"

Liz sucked her teeth. "I might agree with you on that last statement, but I think you're being hasty."

"Well, I'm not. When this deal is done, I'll get my promotion and I won't be on the road as much. Plus, I'll be able to afford a nanny and a rent-a-husband. We'll discuss later. Kiss Dani for me, and tell her I'll give her a call."

Nicole hung up and stepped into the elevator, pulling up the email she'd gotten from the Live to Love adoption agency a few days ago.

Dear Miss Parks,

We are thrilled that you are interested in adopting a child, and thank you for taking the steps to ensure your eligibility. The Greens want you to know that they so enjoyed meeting you and feel that you are a strong candidate as an adoptive parent. Unfortunately, the couple had some concerns about your work schedule, and although you can afford excellent childcare, they have decided to wait for a two-parent home.

Please don't get discouraged. Your child is out there.

As if being single wasn't stigma enough, now young parents were rejecting her. She had a stable job and a killer résumé. What more could she do to make herself a desirable single parent? The agency had suggested that Nicole look into family homes located close to good schools—apparently parents liked that. The three-bedroom Brooklyn house she had been eyeing was still on the market, but she needed some more time to get the down payment together.

But that was before Brazil landed in her lap. She guessed that she could have that deal closed in a few weeks. Then that home and her mini-me, with their live-in French au pair, would be a reality.

Her fairy tale could come true.

The bell dinged, and Nicole strutted out of the elevator.

"Good evening Miss Parks, we are so glad you'll be joining us for dinner."

"Thank you, Anton," she said, recognizing the tall, slim general manager who'd facilitated her hotel check-in hours earlier. Next to him, a hostess smiled. "So am I."

"Monsieur Dechamps hasn't arrived yet, but we'll be happy to seat you, or would you join us at the bar for a complimentary glass of wine while you wait?"

"Say no more, Anton. The bar it is."

"Please follow me."

She heard the dull roar of a packed house and smelled sweet cigars before she even stepped inside the restaurant. The dining room was elegant, with dark wood accents, bistro tables and an oversized bar. Floor-to-ceiling windows allowed patrons to enjoy the busy streets and the boisterous Brazilian nightlife.

Anton helped Nicole onto an empty bar stool near others waiting for their tables, then signaled for the bartender. He half bowed. "I hope your suite is satisfactory?"

"It's very comfortable. And the champagne basket is lovely. Thank you."

"Our pleasure." He gestured toward the barkeep. "Rafe will take care of you. I'll be back to seat you when Monsieur Dechamps arrives."

After perusing the wine list she chose a glass of Beaujolais. The dark ruby liquid poured like silk, and after giving it a good swish in her glass to let the oxygen in, she took a deep inhale, then put it to her lips. It tasted like heaven. Rose, wood, mint and truffle—bursts of flavor danced on her tongue and she mentally logged each one, a habit she'd learned at a summer work–study during college in Bordeaux.

Although she was eager to meet her client, she could feel the tension of her day leaving her body, and she took the opportunity to text her boss—she'd call him tomorrow—and sent several work emails from her phone. She was mid-email when a high-pitched giggling came from the other side of the room.

A young blonde woman in a low-cut minidress walked through a side entrance, but she stopped and turned with an annoyed stance, clearly waiting for someone. Nicole hoped it wasn't more giggling girls.

Just as she was about to turn away, in strolled a tall, dark-haired, starkly handsome man. His square jaw was covered in a trim beard, but it was his eyes that held the most allure. Heavy lidded and thickly lashed, their blue color seemed to resemble translucent cobalt glass. She bet eyes like that glittered when he smiled, but right now he looked bored. And slightly sloshed.

Nicole didn't usually go for the bearded, mountain-man type, but this one, even in a disheveled white button-down shirt, was fine.

And taken. The young woman grabbed his hand and practically pulled him toward the bar.

Turning back to her phone, Nicole noted that Elliot De-champs was ten minutes late, but she didn't stress. Not all cultures took punctuality as seriously as Americans, and sometimes it was nice to let go of those expectations.

She was in a country she'd never explored before, drinking a beautiful red wine. It didn't get much better—

An elbow jostled Nicole's forearm. The couple from across the room was right next to her, sipping champagne and speaking loudly in swift Portuguese. The tipsy woman was having trouble getting onto the stool in her spandex dress. After a few tries, with the help of her boyfriend's outstretched arm, she finally made it.

In celebration, the young woman laughed and shot her elbows out again, knocking over her champagne…and Nicole's wine.

Instantly Nicole's Beaujolais became a pool of dark liquid and broken glass. Heads turned and the bartender sprang into action, gathering white cloths and swiping at the mess, which had begun to travel over the lip of the bar onto Nicole's leg. She jumped from her barstool and stepped away, almost bumping into the blonde, who was no doubt hurrying toward the ladies' room.

Nicole patted down her dress. Thank God she was wearing black, but some wine had gotten on her bare leg.

Suddenly a towel was being dabbed lightly at her thigh.

New York reflexes always on, she grabbed the wrist then tried to hide her shock as she eyed its owner. He was strong, she thought when she felt his arm stiffen and pull back. Dark brows slashed the blue of his eyes when he looked up.

He was even hotter up close.

Chapter 2

"Desculpa," Destin apologized quickly, noting the vice grip the woman had on his wrist. Her wary gaze told him she might not have appreciated his cleaning skills. *"Eu não deveria ter..."*

The woman let go of him and held up her palm. *"Não entendo.* I don't speak Portuguese."

English? Interesting. Just as he was about to explain himself, a birthday procession of sparklers and dessert trays came marching past the bar. Quickly he shot an arm out, pulling the woman closer to shield her from their path.

When the fanfare was across the room, he tried again. "As I was saying, my apologies. I was handing you a towel when I saw an errant drop of wine heading for your knee."

Now in a half circle within his arms, he couldn't believe he hadn't noticed her before. She was strikingly beautiful, with high cheekbones and full lips accentuated by the rich brown of her skin, which was flawless.

Touches of fire still flashed in her eyes, and her body

language told him that she was ready to fend him off if he crossed a line. With a slight bow, he offered her the white cloth and was pleased when he saw the suspicion leave her eyes.

He inspected her sophisticated dress. "I don't believe there are any stains."

"No, I don't think so. Thank you for the towel."

She backed away, her gaze raking over him this time, and he swore he felt the heat of it. He fought an urge to pull her back into his arms. "Allow me to buy you another drink."

"It's fine, really."

She turned, and he watched as she glided back to her open stool. He couldn't tear his attention away from the gentle sway of her hips, those long silky brown legs or her shining black heels.

He was about to insist, but saw that the barkeep had already replenished her glass. Destin took an involuntary step to follow her and then stopped, surprised at his reaction to this mysterious woman. He itched to engage her again. Was he drunk? Of course he was; he'd been drinking all night.

Speaking of which, his drink sat idle on the bar. Taking the seat one stool away from her, Destin propped both of his arms on the bar and took a burning sip of his drink, letting the amber liquid rip down his throat like fire. Relaxing a bit, he opened the top two buttons on his tailored white shirt, hoping his date took her time. She was a handful.

When Thereza's brother had called Destin in a panic, begging him to escort his little sister to the art gala because he could no longer make it, Destin's first answer had been no. He'd already thrown out his invitation. Every year the envelope arrived, addressed to Mr. and Mrs. Destin Dechamps, and every year he stared at the names then tossed it into the trash bin.

He still donated, however. Nina would have wanted that, but he hadn't been able to bring himself to go to the fundraiser since her death. Until this favor. He blamed his father, too, for his lapse in judgment. Destin was supposed to be on a flight to Paris that night, but with their strained relationship, he hadn't been looking forward to it. The gala had seemed like the perfect excuse to cancel.

Now he wished he'd stuck to his first answer. Being at the art gala that afternoon without his wife and seeing their old acquaintances had been jarring. Women who had known Nina for years aggressively invited him to their homes for "dinner." And the men took one look at his date and said they envied his "bachelor lifestyle." Little did they know he'd spent most of his time in his wine cellar, the only place that gave him peace.

And his friend should have told him that little Thereza wasn't so little anymore. The young blonde had spent most of her time at the gala's open bar, and the more she drank, the flirtier she got. She'd tried to climb on top of him in the car ride to the restaurant. He needed to get some food into her. But that wasn't the only reason they were there.

His brother, Elliot, had conveniently forgotten to mention that he was meeting with the real estate lawyer tonight. Destin had found out by accident through their father, of all people—the man who was selling the property out from under them. The thought of Elliot and his father talking behind his back made him want to smash something.

Destin recalled the last conversation he'd had with his father, pleading with him to let him rebuild the winery. They could make the land profitable again. His father refused to listen, saying only that it was in the Dechamps' best interest to sell and infuse the money into the French production. It had turned into a shouting match, with Destin walking out and vowing to do whatever he could to keep the acreage.

That meant keeping the buyers away from the property, and keeping the brokers from doing their jobs…by any means necessary. With the help of some friends, he'd been able to do just that. And this new American real estate lawyer was not going to be an exception. He almost felt bad for the poor bastard. Almost.

Lawyers, he hated them. The yearlong legal battle his father had initiated against Destin, his own son, for sole rights to the signature wine that he'd created still felt like a noose around his throat. Armand Dechamps didn't have just one lawyer; he had a team. And they were vultures. Destin didn't trust lawyers. Not one.

He drew deeply from his whiskey, hoping the meeting hadn't been canceled. His brother was late, not that that was unusual, but he didn't see any lone men who could pass for a smarmy lawyer.

His angry thoughts were interrupted when a silver cone of frites that he had ordered for Thereza arrived. Destin scanned the hallway and saw no sign of her. He hoped she was all right. He popped one into his mouth, then slid them across the bar, offering one to his new friend. "I know Americans love french fries."

She glanced at the fries and then at him, bemused.

With a guilty smile, she took one. "How did you know I was American?"

"Your accent. I've done some business there, in California."

"California is beautiful."

"But you're not from there."

She met his gaze, and a tiny grin touched the corners of her mouth. "No." He watched her lips as she sipped her wine.

Destin waited for her to say more after she put down her glass, but he waited in vain. My, she was reserved. *Maybe she's married*, he immediately thought, but her pink-tipped fingers were bare of jewelry. Could she be traveling alone? He'd heard of American women coming to Brazil for plastic surgery, but couldn't possibly see where she would need any.

"Maybe I should guess?" She only glanced at him. "You're from New York, it's your first time in Brazil, and you're here on a spa vacation."

She smirked and turned to him. "Yes. Yes. And no."

"No vacation? You're here on business? That's too bad," he said after she gave a brief nod. "Brazil is the perfect place for pleasure."

Her brows rose. "Is that why you're here? Pleasure?"

He wished, wondering briefly if her skin was as soft as it looked. "No, I have business, too." He tossed back the rest of his whiskey when he thought of how his brother had tried to hide this meeting from him. Destin couldn't wait to see the look on Elliot's face. "I'm meeting with a lawyer."

"Uh-oh, are you in trouble?"

He smiled. "Nothing like that. I don't like lawyers."

She turned her body toward him, which pleased him. "Really? Why?"

"I've found them to be unfeeling, soulless and greedy. Every last one of them." Her eyes flashed, and he mentally patted himself on the back for holding her attention.

"I know a lot of nice lawyers who would take offense to that."

"Well, I'm sorry for your friends, but I have yet to meet a lawyer who isn't out to get rich while destroying someone else's life."

Her gaze lowered, and she turned her body back toward the bar. "That's unfortunate."

"Unfortunately true." He signaled for another whiskey. "What is it you said you do?"

"Umm… I'm a…yoga instructor."

That made sense. She looked fit.

"Did you just look at my legs?"

Merde. He had. And not just a quick peek; he'd stared a little. "For business purposes only. If I were going to do yoga, I would hire you. You look flexible."

"Excuse me?" Her eyes widened, but she laughed a little, which he liked the sound of.

Mon Dieu, he really was out of practice with women. Where was his whiskey? "I meant, if I were a woman looking for an instructor." He paused. "I think Thereza does yoga," he added quickly, gesturing toward the empty seat. He had no idea if the young blonde did yoga.

"Is your girlfriend okay? She's been in the restroom a while."

"She's probably on the phone. And she's not my girlfriend," he murmured distractedly. The woman turned her head to him slowly and tipped her face toward his. There were sparks in her dark eyes again—exquisite.

"Really? Does *she* know that?" Her icy tone was palpable.

Destin never rose to the touchiness in a woman's voice. In a former life, he had kissed hands, opened doors and led women by the smalls of their backs. His mother had raised him and his brother to be gentlemen. He'd been married to a sweet, stunning lady.

The pain of the memory pulled him back into the present. He was no longer that young man.

And this woman and her commanding tone were stirring something dark in him. Leaning in, he swiveled his amused gaze to her annoyed one. "She knows."

As if on cue, Thereza slid in between them and wrapped her arms around his neck. Her giggles mingled with his audible sigh as he peeled her off him and wrestled her onto her stool, enticing her with the fries.

He peered over Thereza's head at his beautiful new acquaintance, who was now acting like she didn't know him. She sipped her wine, ignoring them, yet he caught the tiniest clench in her jaw. He berated himself for not finding out her name.

Destin saw her head turn toward the entrance and pause. She clutched her small bag and popped off the stool. He watched as she walked toward the crowd of people at the door, curious to see whom she was meeting. Then his thoughts shifted when he spotted Elliot. Finally!

Destin stood and signaled to his brother. The surprise on Elliot's slim face was priceless but short-lived as his attention was diverted by…the yoga instructor?

Chapter 3

Elliot Dechamps strolled into the restaurant, handed his coat to a server and assaulted both of Nicole's cheeks with kisses. His blond hair was slightly longer than in his picture, but he was just as handsome and stylish in a black button-down open at the neck and slim-cut trousers.

"*Enchanté*, Ms. Parks. I hope Anton has taken excellent care of you." He didn't apologize for being late. Instead, his head swiveled toward the bar, and he frowned and nodded at someone. Then he called Anton over and requested that he change their table.

Elliot turned to her. "It looks my brother, Destin, is unexpectedly joining us. And he seems to have brought a friend. I assure you, this is not how we usually do business. My brother can be—" He searched for a word. "Impetuous." With a tight smile, Elliot waved toward the bar.

Nicole's mind ran over the details of the dossier that she had read about the Dechamps brothers. Just a few years out of Oxford, they'd successfully opened a branch of their family's winery. At the time, winemaking in Brazil was still experimental, but they quickly rose to mainstream success. Destin was the eldest and the driving force behind the creation of the wines and the agricultural operation. Elliot was the business mind, and took on the finances and sales.

A fire had taken the winery almost four years ago, along with Destin's wife.

So sad, she thought, as she turned toward the bar and—

No.

Oh, no…

Whiskey in hand, drunk girlfriend struggling to keep up, her lawyer-hating barfly was patting Elliot on the back. Elliot turned to her.

"Miss Parks, my brother, Destin. Destin, Miss Nicole Parks, the attorney from Kingsley's."

Destin slid a glance at his brother, and Nicole was sure he was going to say something smart. Instead, he stretched out his hand, his expression unreadable. "A pleasure to meet you, Miss Parks."

"Lovely to meet you, as well, Monsieur Dechamps." She slipped her palm into the warmth of his hand. Her pulse jumped. She chalked it up to being flustered.

They released each other, and Destin stepped to the side. "And this is Thereza."

Nicole introduced herself to the blonde, who didn't seem to recognize her from the bar at all.

"I thought you were going to Paris tonight," Elliot hissed, pulling Destin off to the side. Nicole eavesdropped as she pretended to look out the bay window, but she could see the brothers from the corner of her eye.

Destin shrugged. "I had another engagement."

Elliot eyed Destin's companion then pursed his lips at Destin. "*Mon Dieu*, Destin, is it really that hard for you to face our father?"

Destin seethed. "I'm leaving tomorrow."

"Good. You need to talk this out."

Destin ignored him.

Evidently satisfied that everyone had met, Elliot took Thereza by the hand and led her toward the table. Destin frowned, his blue gaze boring into Nicole's. Then he offered her his arm for the short walk.

"*You're* the attorney?" he murmured. "No yoga?"

She placed her hand inside his biceps. It felt like steel. "I *do* yoga. I find that it helps me to keep my soul."

He raised a brow at her. "Touché." He led her through the tables. "I supposed my statement was harsh. It just never occurred to me that you were an attorney."

"Well, we come in all shapes and sizes."

"And genders."

"Don't tell me you have a problem with me being a woman."

"Of course not. It's just that you came with such high recommendations that I was expecting a man."

Ooooh, another zinger. It was difficult, but she held her temper. "I'm sorry to disappoint you. But I think you'll find that I can be as unfeeling and greedy as any man, especially when it serves my clients."

Destin's lips twitched. "Oh, I'm not disappointed."

At the table, Elliott moved Thereza's chair back and helped her get seated. Which left Destin to assist Nicole. He smoothly slid her chair forward when she sat, and Nicole glanced at him over her shoulder. No mockery or amusement seemed present in his face.

"*Merci,*" she murmured.

"*À tout moment.*" Anytime.

Elliot requested a bottle of wine, and sent for a flurry of hors d'oeuvres. Their drinks were on the table in seconds, and the small plates of bite-sized appetizers followed promptly.

Surprise must have registered across her face because Elliot leaned over to her with a grin and said, "They know us here. *Saúde*." They all clinked glasses, looking into each other's eyes—no one wanted seven years of bad sex, even if it was an urban legend.

Destin's look was intense when he touched his glass to hers. She took a deep breath, thinking there was probably no such thing as bad sex with him.

Where had that thought come from?

Nicole wrenched her gaze from his. She gave her wine a swirl then inhaled before tasting.

"Wow," Nicole said after her first sip. "That's exceptional."

"It is," Elliott said, his attention shifting to his brother. Destin lowered his whiskey and his eyes.

"A Cab Franc. It's yours, isn't it? A Dechamps?" she asked Elliot.

"It's our father's, yes," Destin answered.

Nicole caught a glimpse of something in his eyes. Regret, maybe? But after another sip of his drink, whatever sadness she'd seen disappeared.

"Hmm. Chili pepper, strawberry, tobacco, licorice." She tapped her tongue on the top of her mouth and sucked in a slow breath. "Leather?" Elliot's eyes widened. "Basil and dark oak from extremely aged barrels. Very earthy."

"Is she right?" Elliot asked his brother excitedly.

Destin was half grinning and studying her as if he'd seen an alien. He glanced at Elliot and slowly nodded.

"How did you do that?" Destin asked Nicole.

"I have a really sensitive palate."

"A supertaster?" Destin asked, astonishment in his tone.

"Mmm-hmm." She nodded shyly.

"Very interesting," Elliot chimed in.

"Not really. It's a nice party trick, but mostly it makes

me a picky eater. Things smell so good and don't always carry through on the taste. It annoys my friends." The brothers laughed, which was the intention, but her mutant taste buds had caused more harm than good when she was a child, especially when her father took over the cooking after her mother passed. If it hadn't been for Cheerios, she wasn't sure she would have survived middle school.

"And your boyfriend? What does he think?" asked Destin.

Was he mocking her again? If he hadn't noticed, his girlfriend had been texting ever since the drinks arrived. Nicole might be single, but at least she had standards.

"I'm not seeing anyone at the moment. So I have all the time in the world to dedicate to the both of you."

"Cheers to that," Destin said. He drained his whiskey and poured himself a glass of the Cab Franc.

Elliot narrowed his eyes and cocked his head at his brother, then turned to her. "I must say, I had no idea you'd be so beautiful in person."

Warning bells chimed in Nicole's head at the offhand comment. Even Destin frowned. Ever the professional, Nicole gave him a practiced smile, still unsure if he was flirting or just being very French.

"*Merci*. For the compliment and the opportunity to let me facilitate your sale. I understand the land has been untouched for quite some time. Are you certain it can't be salvaged?" she asked softly. Elliot froze, and he gazed across the table. She turned to Destin, who was fingering the stem of his glass, and spoke carefully. "I hope you don't think I'm being insensitive to your family tragedy. I'm so sorry for your loss and want you to know that our company has many resources that could help you rebuild. I would be remiss if I didn't present all of the options."

Destin seemed far away for a moment. Then he held his glass up to the lit candle in the middle of their table and studied the dark burgundy liquid. His gaze flicked to her over the rim.

"Wine making is an art, and in France it's about timing. The seasons determine when the grapes ripen and when to harvest. But in Brazil, there are three hundred days of sunshine. The vines never stop producing, and harvesting can happen at any time. That's why Elliot and I came here to make our mark." More food arrived and Destin paused, pushing a few of the plates toward Nicole. "Please, eat. Let's see what your palate can handle." His smile was genuine, and she couldn't help but grin back. She started in on the spiced churrasco and the smoked octopus.

Destin watched her take a bite, then raised one brow in a silent question. *How is it?* She licked her lips and grinned in answer. Her smile slowly fell when he turned to Thereza, who began to eat one of the pork ribs with her fingers. Nicole almost felt bad for her. Her minimal English meant she couldn't follow the conversation. In between texts, the blonde had flipped her hair and flashed her eyes, anything to get Destin to look her way.

He'd been polite, offering her wine and food, making sure she was comfortable, but Nicole could tell this was a one-sided love match. Destin wasn't into Thereza, which provided Nicole with some inexplicable inner satisfaction.

She had to ask herself why she cared.

"Brazil is an exciting country," Elliot said, interrupting her thoughts. "But it can be a savage and lawless place. Young boys can get into a lot of trouble here." Elliot smirked, as if he indulged in trouble frequently. "Our winery was successful for a time, maybe too successful. Someone broke in and knocked a lit oil lamp over. The fire took everything."

"That's awful," she said cautiously, her gaze going back and forth between the men.

Destin didn't look up; instead, he ran his hand back

and forth over the white tablecloth. "The irrigation pipes were ruined, and the soil is no longer suitable. And, of course, our production facilities were destroyed. Rebuilding would be a waste of time and money," he said, trailing off into a whisper.

Nicole swallowed back her own memories of losing close family members. Her mother had been the first to go, her degenerative heart condition taking her when Nicole was only ten. Then her father's constant drinking and liver cirrhosis took him not long after. By the time Nicole was twelve, the only relative she had left was her grandmother.

Nicole recognized that this man was still in pain. She pushed the octopus plate his way, but he shook his head and smiled at her in gratitude.

He had a nice mouth, she thought. And his eyes seemed to glitter.

"Well, I've brought inquiries from several prospective buyers with me that we can discuss. They seem to agree that there is a lot of opportunity in Brazil. There is an oil tycoon who…"

Destin rose suddenly. "I think I should take Thereza home. Please, continue without us."

Elliot rose. "You're sure you can't stay?" His gaze flicked to Nicole, then back to his brother.

"No. Unfortunately," Destin murmured.

"You're still off to Paris in the morning?" Elliot asked, grasping his brother's outstretched hand.

Destin nodded as they shook goodbye, then he turned to Nicole. "It was lovely to meet you Miss Parks. I'm sure you'll take good care of us." He stared into her eyes as he took her hand and kissed the backs of her fingers.

She grinned and studied his face. "Safe travels."

Thereza smiled and waved goodbye before turning for the exit.

Nicole turned back to Elliot, but Destin's departing broad shoulders monopolized her peripheral vision until he strode out of the restaurant. She told herself that the sinking feeling she was experiencing wasn't disappointment. Surely she didn't care that he was taking his girlfriend home. She wasn't attracted to him; it was more like a misplaced sympathy. She felt sorry for him. That was all. Anyway, he was off to Paris. She'd probably never see him again.

"Please excuse Destin, it took him a while to accept the idea of selling. This was his dream, and it's hard for him to let it go. Even after what happened."

Nicole understood letting go of dreams. Her thoughts turned toward the adoption, and she hoped she wouldn't have to let that go.

One more bottle of wine, two desserts and one espresso later, Nicole and Elliot had hashed out the expectations for the sale.

"So, do you have any more questions for me? Anything else you want to know?" Nicole asked, taking the last bite of her acai sorbet.

Elliot thought for a moment. "Whatever we missed tonight, I'm sure we'll think of tomorrow."

"Tomorrow?"

"*Bien sûr.* I'll be giving you a tour of the land. I can't wait to show you Dechamps and Rio Grande."

Chapter 4

Brazil's blinding afternoon sun rose high above a vast, unkempt field and beat down on Destin's back as he squatted inside the remnants of a burned and crumbling building. Though he kept his dark head bent, his thin T-shirt did little to shield him from the sun's hot rays, and he shifted himself into the triangle of shade provided by the partial wall blackened by fire patterns. He swiped at the sweat beaded on his neck and shooed away Magnus, his German shepherd, as he cleared rocks and sticks from the piles of ash, brick and stone that peppered the dirt floor.

He'd found things in the rubble before: a hairbrush, broken crystal decanters, a melted tobacco pipe. But he never found what he was truly looking for—answers. *What had happened to his life?* Each artifact he found felt like a piece of a puzzle that still eluded him. His wife and everything they'd worked for had disappeared in one night.

He tossed a rock at the charred wall, wishing he could as easily toss the guilt. It had been his idea to start a branch of Dechamps in Brazil, and he and Nina had taken such pride in their new home. They'd had high hopes to build something here, the way his father had done in France. But she was gone now, and it was all his fault.

Yet the thought of letting it go made his stomach turn. *Nicole Parks.* Her dark eyes had been haunting him since he left the restaurant the night before. Even after he'd dropped Thereza off at her apartment, refusing to have a nightcap—despite her offer and the suggestive way she'd kissed him goodbye.

His mind replayed his interaction with the feisty attorney over and over. She had a sharp wit and self-assurance. Her poise and direct way of speaking were unnerving, he decided, as if weighing the pros and cons. He'd bet she was stubborn, too. An inner voice told him that those qualities probably made her a good lawyer. A second inner voice reminded him that Nina had been just as bold.

When Nicole had mentioned potential buyers the night before, Destin found he couldn't listen to the possibility that his failed aspirations might become a success story for someone else. Jumping out of his seat was a reflex, one he had instantly regretted. Once he'd stood, he found that, as much as he wanted to leave the conversation, he hadn't wanted to leave Nicole's presence.

The attorney held a certain fascination for him that he couldn't deny. She was clearly intelligent, and at times had been rather charming. A classic beauty, she'd worn little makeup at dinner, which was a refreshing change from the heavily made-up women at the restaurant. She was tall, about five foot seven, he guessed, and curvy. He had a sneaking suspicion that she might fit against his tall frame quite nicely.

And she was a supertaster. What were the odds of that? He imagined taking her to his workspace in the cellar, letting her taste the wines that had been aging in their barrels since before the fire. Feeding her the foods and desserts he'd paired them with.

Bouncing another rock against the wall, he rebuked himself for those thoughts. Nicole Parks was working for his father. No matter how intriguing she was, he had to make sure that she didn't succeed.

His soot-covered fingertips swiped at a rock, uncovering a glint of silver. He dug out the small rectangular shape, rubbed it, popped off the top then closed it shut. A lighter. He weighed it in his hand and flipped it around, using his thumbs to clear the dirt. An engraved D became visible. Clutching the lighter hard in his palm, he pulled his fist to his lips and closed his eyes as if in prayer.

He slipped it into his pocket, slapped his hands on his cargo pants, grabbed his shotgun and left the forsaken structure. His four-legged companion loped ahead of him as his boots trod hard through the brush of the surrounding forest, his shotgun in one hand and a small bouquet of wildflowers in the other. The dog waited for him at their destination, a small gravesite with two markers.

He placed the flowers on the graves, and they mingled with the dead petals of the previous bouquet.

Thunder cracked overhead. Clouds had darkened and gathered, suggesting a storm, the quick and fierce kind that Rio Grande was famous for.

They turned back, moving quickly, he and the dog noticing the mass evacuation of the forest inhabitants. Raising his gun, he shot and missed a large brown rabbit when it bounced high in the air. Even the dog couldn't catch it. Clearing the trees, the pair moved swiftly toward the wine cellar, a high stone structure with a wide wooden door. Just before they entered, the dog barked and turned toward the vastness of the untended plantation. Destin cocked his gun, listening. He heard a car approach in the distance.

* * *

Spectacular. The word resonated over and over in Nicole Parks's mind as she looked out over the countryside of Rio Grande and navigated the winding mountain road in her rental SUV. Elliot had offered to hire her a driver, but she enjoyed the freedom that renting a car gave her. According to her GPS, she was just twenty minutes outside of Porto Alegre and about ten minutes from the Dechamps winery.

Miles and miles of exuberant nature grew out from the knolls and stretched far into the distance. She eased up on the gas pedal so she could take longer glimpses at waterfalls, rushing streams and small canyons—areas completely undisturbed by human intervention.

In contrast, each cliff-side wind of the road allowed a peek into the valley at the multicolored box homes of the favelas. They sat one on top of the other, climbing up the bottom of the mountain like steps and sprawling around the city like a horseshoe. From what she'd read, the favelas were riddled with crime. From her vantage point, they seemed calm and beautiful.

On the map, the digital dot of her car looked like it was marching up and over a cliff. She had to be close. Yet there were no road markers, and the farther she got up the mountain, the denser the overgrowth of vegetation became, so much so that the sun had to fight to get through. She wondered if anyone would find her if she mysteriously disappeared; she hadn't passed a car or seen a soul for miles.

Minutes later her GPS spoke in a soothing, robotic tone over the radio and air conditioner, telling her to turn right in a quarter mile. She crept farther and farther forward, trying to spot a gate or a gap in the greenery. There was nothing—but then she saw it, a spike with a tarnished brass top wound by dirt and vines. A driveway marker, perhaps? She nosed her SUV through the brush, and sure enough, it gave way. A jagged road became visible, and she followed it until the overgrowth became like a wall. She rolled to a stop, excited to explore before Elliot arrived.

She checked her appearance in the rearview: makeup still intact, ponytail smooth, white button-down shirt tucked into a burgundy pencil skirt. She let out a nervous yelp when her phone rang on the seat next to her. Surprised that she still had reception in the middle of nowhere, she placed a hand over her racing heart and lifted the phone to her ear.

"Hello?"

"You made it?" She pictured Senior Global Real Estate Advisor Gustavo Escarra swiveling around in his giant leather desk chair overlooking Central Park.

"Hey, boss. Yeah, I'm at the winery now. Elliot Dechamps is meeting me here in a few minutes."

Nicole filled Gus in on her dinner the night before. "They seem eager to get rid of the place." Silence. "Hello? Gus?" She sighed, wondering if the call had dropped.

"Nicole?"

"I'm here. You cut out for a second."

"I said, how does the place look?" Gus asked.

"I haven't gone in yet, but it's already an overgrown mess. We may have to persuade the client to spend some money landscaping. I'm talking bulldozers, the works."

"Well, this might be worth it. We're going to have to get appraisals on everything from the irrigation pipes to the number of dead vines. And quickly. We have a lot of interested buyers who want to see this place immediately."

"I'm on it."

"And I don't have to tell you that your promotion will be waiting here when you close this deal."

"Consider it done," Nicole said nonchalantly. But she began to feel that rush of a potential sale, and her new life with a big office and a kid in her lap dangled in front of her. "Oh, and say hi to Don for me. What's he working on, by the way?"

Gustavo chuckled, always finding the rivalry between Nicole and Don amusing. Don was a smooth-talking Chi-town native who liked to pitch himself against Nicole's New York street swag. "Don is taking care of a celebrity home sale. I'll tell him you said hello."

Nicole's eyes lit up. Celebrities were the worst clients! "Just so you know, I am going to rub this in his face."

"Have at it," Gustavo said. She could hear him smile, and her skin pricked with more than just excitement. She'd learned much from Gustavo and she admired him, probably a little more than she should.

Okay, she had a crush on her boss.

He was about ten years older and stood over six feet tall with a nice body. And he looked great in a suit. Well groomed, handsome, and of course, wealthy—with a few homes around the globe.

He was perfect. Everything she wanted in a man.

And married to some former Miss Universe pageant winner who was also the mother of his three beautiful children.

Whatever. My Gustavo is out there. Somewhere. Right?

The question brought up images of Destin. She couldn't tell if he was a player or a perfect gentleman. Was he a chauvinist or a boyish joker? One thing was certain: he was damaged goods. And as much as he tried to mask it, those moments when his eyes had darkened during their discussion about the land spoke volumes.

Again she told herself that her interest in him was derived from pity. She'd lost family too. Except she'd gone back to her hotel room after dinner and found herself thinking of Destin's intense blue gaze and his mischievous smile. She liked his size and saw herself in the crook of his arm. What would his beard feel like against her cheek when he kissed her?

Get a grip! No. She refused to be attracted to him. Broken men couldn't be fixed. She'd tried and failed too many times. She was thankful he wasn't interested in the sale of the land. She doubted she'd see him again.

But still, she wondered if he'd made love to Thereza that night, and felt the smallest twinge of jealousy at the thought.

Grabbing her keys and the old black-and-white picture of the Dechamps winery, Nicole jumped out of the SUV to search for an entrance. The formidable vegetation gave no hint of a door. For all she knew, she was at the wall of Jurassic Park. Her small heels sank into the dirt and she worked to pull them out, her skirt hindering her movements, only to have them sink back in.

Exasperated, she opened the back of the car and rummaged through her tote bag for her flip-flops, but found only her blazer and wallet. She'd really misjudged this little adventure. Shoving her keys and phone in her bag, she slung it over her shoulder, stepped carefully around the other side of the car and squeezed herself through an opening between two large palm trees.

Nicole definitely wasn't in New York anymore. Dead leaves rustled, something chirped overhead and the trees seemed to bend toward her. She freaked, moving forward as fast as she could, following a natural path, dodging twigs coming at her head and swatting at leaves that scraped her arms. She stumbled forward into a clearing, caught herself and then squinted up at her surroundings. She recognized the skeletal remnants of the winery instantly.

She held up the black-and-white picture, locating the main house, and studied the photo before dropping her arm. The fire had taken half of the front building. Rooms were roofless and exposed. She noticed the other vine-covered buildings that were spread out farther back—burned, crumbling and neglected. Behind them in the far distance were rows upon rows of gnarled and broken grapevines. The massive trees in the picture, now decayed chunks in the ground, must have been how the flames traveled from one building to the next.

During her summer in France, she'd enjoyed waking early to help with the harvest, walking between the vines, breaking for a four-course lunch feast with her host family. Love and laughter were served with the pinot noir. This place hadn't seen that in a long time. It was desolate, scarily so.

She snapped some pictures on her phone, noticing in one the dark sky in the corner. Tipping her head back, she saw clouds race by—some dark and thick, others white as cotton balls—but the sun seemed to scare them away. The surrounding trees swayed hard, then stopped. The air smelled like fall leaves. It was a bluebird day, hot as hell, though. She swore the humidity was getting thicker.

She took in the seclusion of the plantation—a great selling point. Again, the trees rustled and a loud thud startled her, as if something heavy had fallen, and it occurred to her that she was in a foreign country, in the wilderness, *alone*. She listened carefully for people or, God forbid, animals. Being a city kid, she was tough, but wild things were not her forte.

She turned to go back to the car, suddenly aware of a large shadow rising overhead. Thunder cracked, and the darkened sky flashed with lightning. A droplet, followed by a few more, fell on Nicole's head and shoulders. She lunged forward to find her path back to the car, catching her heel in the already-soft ground. The sky became darker still, and the clouds unleashed. Her ears filled with the rush of the water within the surrounding trees, and rain pelted her eyes. She again tried to move forward, but her exit path had disappeared in the downpour.

A dog barked from not too far away. Through the rain, she could see its black-and-caramel form standing alert inside the open doorway of a small shack. A shack with a roof!

She wanted to run there, but what if the dog wasn't friendly? Or had rabies? The dog barked again and took off into the rain. She rushed forward toward the open door, her heels sliding all over the place, but she pushed on. Breathless and soaked, she felt the cool air on her skin as she made it inside the shadowed doorway. She swiped at her eyes, blinking rapidly, and ran straight into a body.

The scream she let out could only be described as bloodcurdling. She shoved her back against the wall and focused on a dark silhouette across from her. The figure moved into a shaft of light.

Her breath caught when she recognized Destin's concerned blue eyes.

"Destin! Oh, my God, you scared me."

"Nicole! What the…are you all right? That fallen branch didn't get a piece of you, did it?" His voice sounded melodic over the pounding of the rain, and it took her a second to register that he had asked her a question.

"I—I don't think so." She didn't even know one had fallen near her.

"May I?" Without hesitating, he stepped closer, his head bent toward hers, and ran light fingers from her neck over her shoulder, carefully scanning for nicks and scrapes. She shivered, but it wasn't from cold.

She watched his every movement, silently noting his perfectly straight nose and full lips. Michelangelo himself could have carved his cheekbones. His gaze stopped at the V of her soaked white shirt. He looked up and quickly stepped back.

"I don't think you're injured!" he shouted as the rain increased.

She slumped against the wall and tried to steady her breathing. Her lungs felt heavy with moist air. "What are you doing here? I thought you were heading to France."

The thunder crack was deafening, and lightning streaked the sky. Destin shook his head. "Not in this weather. I came to make sure the drains were open—if not, the cellar could flood. What are you doing here?"

"I'm meeting Elliot."

Destin shook his head rapidly. "I spoke to my brother this morning. He was going to call you to cancel."

Nicole lifted her phone. Sure enough, a voicemail symbol popped up.

"I'll leave. Just let me catch my breath. My heart is racing. It's so humid," she said, pulling at her shirt, wincing when she saw one of her buttons pop off and hit the ground. Quickly she pinched her shirt over her cleavage. When she looked up, Destin's gaze darted away. He cleared his throat.

"You can't drive in this, Nicole. You don't know these roads."

Just then, a streak of wet fur came bursting into the doorway, and the dog shook water all over them both. Nicole jumped and let a loud shriek. On shaky legs, she stepped away and heard an audible *snap*. Just as her heel gave way and her body lurched toward the floor, she was suddenly airborne and hoisted into strong arms.

"Whoa," Destin said, his lips inches from hers. "I got you."

Chapter 5

"Welcome to the wine cellar," he gritted out, quickly descending the stairs with her cradled in his arms. "Let's take a look at that ankle." Destin gently set her down on a bench next to a long sturdy table, slipped off her shoe and bent over her already swollen ankle. Her gaze darted around the disorganized room, then landed on her savior—in a black long-sleeved Henley with the top three buttons undone, a light smattering of dark chest hair peeking out, cargo pants and hard-worn boots. His damp hair curled and spiked around his ears. She itched to smooth it down.

He pushed up his sleeves, and she watched his forearm muscles flex. She wondered if he worked out, then mentally shook her head. Those weren't gym-honed muscles. He was a vintner. A farmer. Working shirtless in the sun. Doing manly stuff like lifting barrels and digging ditches. At least, he used to.

She got a little overwhelmed at how very male he looked squatting in front of her. Then he touched her, his large hands gentle as he ran his thumb around the swelling, testing and pushing at the tender skin.

Any pain was overshadowed by the rush of heat that suddenly strained between her legs. The unexpected sensations had her lifting her foot away slightly. He raised his head but kept hold and lifted his other palm to her calf for support.

"Does this hurt?" His brows were high with worry.

What could she say? *No, but could you please run your hands all over my body?*

"No, but—" She hissed. "Oww," she said when Destin bent her ankle inward. She wiggled her toes, testing that it wasn't broken. And became more and more embarrassed that he was staring at her foot so intently. Thank God her pedicure was still intact.

"Just a sprain, I think," he said, lowering her foot to the floor. Carefully, he placed her shoe back on and she winced, but not from pain—the heel of her shoe had completely broken off.

"Uh! My Jimmy Choos," Nicole whined, then instantly regretted sounding like a Kardashian. But those were expensive. *Calm down*, she told herself. She could get them fixed on 57th Street. Ira wasn't just a cobbler; he was a magician. She'd need the broken heel, though.

The wet mongrel that had started this mess chose that moment to walk by, and he was chewing on something small and cone shaped. The scruffy mutt lowered himself onto the concrete floor and chomped down, right into her heel. Nicole's eyes widened, and she began snapping her fingers.

"No! Drop it! Come here. Come here!"

He lifted and cocked his head, then ignored her and proceeded to tear at the leather.

Still crouched, Destin twisted around. "Looks like Magnus likes Jimmy Choos, too." He chuckled, and the sensual sound brought Nicole out of her haze. But before she knew what was happening, Destin slipped off her other shoe, tore off the heel with his bare hand and tossed it right between Magnus's paws.

"Now your shoes will be even heights. We'll get you another pair," he said with a smirk as her jaw fell open. Suddenly everything was just too much. She should put this guy in his place. She should put Elliot in his place! She should bill this little visit by the hour. She should—

Destin stood abruptly, his hand on his hips and his pelvis right in her line of sight. She blinked. What was she thinking?

"I don't have any ice," he murmured as he looked around the room. "You'll just have to keep it elevated." Sliding another bench close to her, he propped up her leg. She focused on keeping her skirt down as it bunched up to midthigh, the rip in the fabric straining wide. "How does that feel?"

"It's fine. Really…" As in *really attractive*, maybe even more so in his casual clothes than he'd been in a jacket last night. His face was all angular planes and strong jaw. That perfect brow remained in a frown, unsatisfied. He stepped around her and disappeared through a door she hadn't noticed.

She took a moment to scan her surroundings. Empty light sockets dominated the walls, but a few strategically placed bulbs illuminated the room with a soft warmth. Stone walls and high ceilings were accented by long archways and dusty cherrywood beams.

The wine cellar was in her files, but there was no mention of it being in working order. She assumed it had been above ground and destroyed. Across the room, white sheets were draped over other furniture. The ghostly round outlines suggested bar tables that probably once sat in a lounge area. Glass display cabinets were empty. Oil lamps sat unused on the shelves, and wires poked from the ceiling, suggesting a chandelier had hung over the table at one time.

Sitting and dining rooms in a wine cellar weren't uncommon, especially in new wineries. They could have had tastings there, or offered tours and events. The winery in Bordeaux hosted weddings in their cask room.

She leaned against the lip of the dining table and ran a hand over the smooth wood. Could the furnished cellar be a selling point? Maybe, depending on who the client was. It could be a storage room, a novelty playroom of some sort, even a fun office space. She could come up with a ton of ideas.

She made a mental note to ask Destin if he was planning on keeping the furniture.

Scrapes and shuffles behind her echoed from the open doorway to her left. Bracing herself on her arms, she leaned over and peered over the threshold. The large chamber accommodated stacked oak barrels and a wall lined with black corked bottles. Nicole felt a shiver of excitement. The cask room—where the wines matured in oak barrels before bottling.

She twisted farther, trying to see the expanse, only to be met with a wall of chilled air. Goosebumps tightened her skin, and she started to pull back but stopped when she noticed one barrel was standing upright and away from the rest. A spigot was tapped into the top, a small empty wine glass off to the side. PH strips were strewn on the spigot lid.

During her time in France, Nicole had participated in many batch tests where acidity levels were checked before fermentation and again at bottling time. Titration kits were preferred, but PH strips were good for a quick read. Could there be wine in there still? Since the fire had happened four years ago, she supposed there could be several batches about to reach maturity.

Nicole's brain began running through the property file she'd read over several times. Nowhere did the asset sheet mention viable wines. She was sure of it. Everything on the property should have been calculated into the property value. She made a mental note to check again.

She heard Destin's boots before she saw him. Unaware he was being watched, he walked to a corner of the room and then tapped a few buttons on a wall panel. A fine mist—so fine you could barely see it—lifted from three or four tiny sprinklers placed strategically around the casks.

No way. She'd heard of the innovative cooling system designed to control humidity, but had never seen it in action.

Oh, yeah. There was wine in there. Lots and lots of wine.

With his back still to her, Destin bent over and placed his hand in the mist, waving his fingers to catch the temperature. Her thoughts jumbled a bit. She was unable to do anything but stare. Her gaze ran over his back.

She whipped herself to a proper sitting position. What was happening—had it been that long since she'd been with a man? Her last boyfriend had been eight months ago. And now she was laid up underground in another country with a French wine lover.

Why was she thinking about this? Was this the beginning of Stockholm syndrome?

Destin shut the door behind her. He presented several wool blankets, and with those gentle hands, he tucked a folded mound under her ankle. Then he unfolded another and, shaking it out high into the air, let it float down over her body.

"There, you're still a bit damp. These will keep you warm," Destin said, tucking the fabric around her legs, making a cocoon from her upper body down and around her feet. Subtle scents of laundered wool filled her nose, again giving her the feeling that those blankets hadn't remained there untouched for four years. The cellar was a valid asset.

But all thoughts were erased when he stroked her thigh with his palm.

She found herself slightly lifted onto one side as he wrapped her in the blanket like a burrito. He made painstaking efforts to tuck her in, leaning over her body, bunching the blanket under her legs and behind her back. His soft hair brushed her nose, and the clean scent had her insides dancing.

She was achingly aware of the man in front of her. She didn't move on account of his handiwork, but the most intimate part of her was screaming to get out.

It was unlike her, this physical reaction to someone she barely knew, and yet here she was, lusting after his body like a teenager who'd just hit puberty. Honestly, she'd seen plenty of hot men. Had slept with…well, who was counting, but she was in her late thirties and dated maybe one or two guys a year, which equated to…oh, God. Well, she'd seen a man before, anyway, and this one was average.

He lowered himself onto another bench across from her, glancing at the dog before bring his blue eyes up to hers.

Okay. He wasn't average.

"Thank you. Again. I, uh… I'm a little embarrassed," Nicole said, searching for conversation, hoping to distract herself from his allure.

"Don't be. I'm just glad you're all right. You could have gotten stuck on the roads. Are you warm enough?"

"Yes. These are bulletproof," she joked, pulling her arms out and tucking the blanket under her armpits. "I'm already getting hot."

"Good. The temperature stays pretty cool down here,

so being wet isn't a good idea. Trust me. It's not the first time I've gotten stuck in here." Destin looked around, as if trying to think of things to say.

After a long moment, Nicole spoke on autopilot. "So, this is the wine cellar."

His nod was slow, and he had a sad look in his eyes. "This *was* the wine cellar."

Her heart twisted. "You have a lot of furniture down here. Did you do tours?"

"We had plans for tours and tastings, as well as a sustainable dining experience in the future. Everything was to be farm to table, from the wine to the produce—we had just started a garden. My neighbor, Bruno, has a free-range animal farm. He would have provided the meat."

"Free range?"

"Meaning they have shelter but no cages. He has acres, and the animals roam freely within his land borders." He chuckled. "They've been known to get spooked and break out on days like this. After a particularly bad storm, we found a herd of his cows grazing on our lawn."

Nicole thought of New York during a storm. The subways slowed, cabs were impossible to find and umbrellas were instruments of death to pedestrians who couldn't bob and weave. Maybe being in a wine cellar with a handsome man wasn't so bad, especially when he laughed like that.

"How often do these storms happen?"

"Four to six times a year, I'd say—mostly when the seasons change. Nina, my wife, was good at planning for disasters. Hence the blankets." His gaze stayed on the table for a minute. Then he jumped up and grabbed a leather backpack from the floor. He took out a wrapped sandwich. "How about some food? It's a Bauru—roast beef, tomato, mozzarella and pickles on French bread. A classic Brazilian sandwich. We can share."

She hadn't realized she was hungry until he mentioned

food. "Sounds delicious. Do you always carry lunch in your bag?"

"Only if I know I'll be busy. I'll warm it for us. There's a lightly stocked kitchenette with a hot plate through that archway."

"Nice. It's like a combination wine cellar and bomb shelter. Our buyers will definitely be into this."

Destin lowered his gaze and swallowed whatever he was going to say. He just smiled, but it didn't reach his eyes.

"I'm sorry if I interrupted something important," she said quickly.

He glanced at the cask room, then to her. "No, just cleaning it out." There was a strain in his voice that said otherwise.

He wasn't ready for this sale, her instincts told her. It wasn't the first time she had come up against reluctant sellers. But something was different. She couldn't put her finger on it; maybe it was because of the tension between him and Elliot at dinner the night before, but something was off.

He placed the sandwich on the table and fished in his bag again. He gripped a bottle of water and a Red Bull in one hand. "And I have these."

"You really are a lifesaver." She reached for the water and he slid it across the table. She twisted off the cap and drank deeply.

"You need to save some of that."

She stopped and pulled the bottle from her lips. "Why?"

"We may be here a while."

"How long is a while?"

He strode to the stairway door and pulled it open. Magnus, thinking his master was leaving, sauntered to his side. The rain was a roar, and the humidity was palpable. Destin closed the door and turned toward Nicole.

"I can hear it," she said. "It's bad. I hope I have damage insurance on that car."

"I hope you do, too." He grimaced. "We may be here overnight."

Her eyes widened. "Are you joking?" She looked around. "Where would we sleep? And I have clients tomorrow afternoon."

His eyes changed. "That quickly?"

"Yes. That's why I needed a tour today." He looked shocked, or rather, devastated. "You don't look happy."

He blinked, then turned his back to her. His voice came out in a half whisper. "I am. Of course I am."

She wasn't convinced. "Destin, you can voice your concerns. The transition is always difficult for the seller."

Destin turned and fixed a cold blue gaze on her. "I look forward to the sale, Miss Parks. The faster the better."

Chapter 6

Destin strode to the kitchenette and fired up the hot plate, his mind racing. She wasn't supposed to get this far. The previous agents had never seen the inside of the cellar—he'd seen to that.

Destin replayed the words his father had said to him at the beginning of the year. Armand Dechamps had stood at the head of the board of directors table, his hair graying, leaning on a gold-tipped cane, but still formidable. His business advisors surrounded him.

"Between your start-up costs, the insurance company refusing to process our claim and the property taxes on idle land, Brazil is financially draining us. We have to sell now, unless you have another idea to make revenue." Armand had narrowed his gaze. "Are you sure there is no more wine in that cellar, Destin?"

Stunned and speechless at the turn of the discussion, he'd looked at the man who'd taught him how to tell time by the sun's placement in the sky and simply said no. He'd lied; there was wine, and remembering how his father tried to take it from him, he didn't feel bad about lying.

Destin knew his father's techniques like the back of his hand, and he'd applied everything he knew to make the awarding-winning Cab Franc for Dechamps France. But he'd experimented in Brazil, making his own signature Cab Franc—lighter bodied, ruby red, tart berry flavors with ethereal hints of earth, rose and violet.

Dechamps Brazil ended up in *Wine Spectator* magazine, was featured in blogs across the world and began to win awards of its own. Local businesses were supplied with Dechamps wines at a discount and every week they were sold out at the Saturday market.

Wine was for the people, and they implemented a direct-to-consumer subscription plan. After three years up and running, Dechamps Brazil surpassed expectations.

And that's when their father tried to shut them down.

His father's jealousy was a blow Destin hadn't seen coming. Suddenly he'd found himself in a legal battle with his father over the rights to his own wines. The French team had taken over production of Destin's signature Cab Franc, and distribution was to be solely commercial—no more direct to consumer.

Destin and Elliot had fought to split from Dechamps France, but under their contract, anything produced under the Dechamps umbrella belonged to their father. Even if they split, they couldn't take the wine with them. Even Elliot, the one who was so much like their deceased mother, hadn't been able to reason with Armand.

Destin had been prepared to go to court. He'd never gotten the chance. The fire took everything he'd loved, except the cellar.

For months after Nina's funeral, he'd eaten little, said little and seen no one. The château where he lived now had originally been a place for their father to stay when visiting. Destin had spent six months on that couch, grieving. Food would magically appear in the kitchen—Elliot's doing, although they never spoke about it.

One morning he'd walked the three miles to the winery and seen the damage—scorched earth, melted metal and crumbling stone. The air had still smelled charred and ash had still been blowing in the wind. But he'd noted that the outer, more dense foliage had begun to regrow. Shining green leaves were poking out of the wreckage and quivering on shaky new stems. The terroir had lost water and nutrients, but the land still lived.

With renewed hope, he'd run through the thousand vines. Once vibrant, all were broken, wilted and black. As far as he could see, no grape had survived. He'd worked his fingernails into the branches, looking for life on one after another. And found nothing.

Tears had blinded him when his gaze dropped to a dead vine in the very last row. Gnarled and bent, at first glance it seemed to have nothing left, and the vine had somehow twisted itself half out of its planting hole. Destin had run his fingertips down the rough stem, then stopped when they met a yellow, half-gone leaf. Under the leaf had been one small, rotting grape. Again, with his fingertips, he'd picked at the gray bark on the curved underside of the vine and peeled it back. It was green. A healthy, bright green.

He'd checked every vine, marking those with potential to live and immediately replanting them in the untouched soil behind the cellar. There was no man-made irrigation there, and the place had had to be cleared in order to let in the sun. And sixty of the eighty-six vines he'd replanted had survived.

Now, everything was done by hand, from the de-stemming to the bottling. He didn't even have a label. Only two batches were about to reach maturity. With the help of a few of their old farm hands, they were on track to produce about two thousand bottles this year.

And it was on the strength of those batches that he'd planned to rebuild. But he had to do it alone, since Elliot had moved on to other business ventures, and was afraid of their father's wrath. His bother had promised to keep Destin's plans a secret.

It had taken almost a year, but Destin had amassed a small team of investors—friends from school and business contacts who were ready to help—and with a relatively small upfront investment of his own, he could replace the production equipment. He just needed to secure the land from his father.

It was his one shot to keep what was rightfully his. And he wasn't going to let anyone get in the way.

He had been checking the vines when the sky opened up, and then Nicole had come crashing through the doorway.

The sight of her, drenched and out of breath, had burned itself into his brain. She had been light as a feather in his arms, her skin hot and slippery from the rain. He'd breathed in the subtle scent of coconut from her hair. Her shirt had gaped from a popped button, and he'd glimpsed her full cleavage, which was barely restrained by a brown satin bra. He wondered if she wore panties to match, then pictured her nude, before deciding that line of thinking wasn't helping.

She was too capable, too unpredictable…too beautiful.

Deep in his thoughts, Destin placed the sandwich on the hot plate and accidentally burned his knuckle. He hissed and popped the singed flesh into his mouth.

"Do you need help back there?" Nicole called out.

Destin realized he had been hiding for several minutes. "No, I just…" *Was thinking of making love to you and almost burned off my fingers.* Destin spied a lone mason jar of stew he'd left there a few weeks ago. "I found some stew for us." He grabbed a small pot, emptied the mason jar into it and placed it on the hot plate alongside the Bauru.

Quietly, he peered around the corner into the main room. Nicole was checking her ankle, the blanket shoved aside and her lower leg visible. She swatted at Magnus, who was inspecting her every movement with his wet nose. The dog planted his butt on the floor, and she praised him with cute noises as she lightly stroked his head.

She had no gloss on her full lips, and her eye makeup had washed off, leaving small black smudges under her eyes. Her hair was still damp and was transforming into tousled waves. And those legs…even the night before, they'd had him mesmerized. Recalling the softness of her calf and the rip in her skirt, he cursed under his breath. Those legs were going to be the end of him.

Dammit—he had no time for sexual attraction, especially under the circumstances, but there was something about this woman. She was smart, ambitious and knowledgeable about wine, which almost made her a threat.

He just wanted her gone. For the sake of his wine and— he rubbed at his knuckle—his sanity.

Being trapped in a small space with a handsome man would have been great if that small space had been a hot tub, but the stone walls and the damp, cold air of the wine cellar, although possibly romantic at one time, felt more like a dungeon. Nicole was wrapped in blankets, her bare leg awkwardly stretched out onto the bench. Her tote bag was wet and crumpled in the middle of the table. She'd lost a button on her shirt, and she refused to think about what her hair was doing.

She blew out an annoyed breath. Why was she thinking about her appearance? Destin was her client, not a prospective boyfriend. And he had a girlfriend. She recalled watching Destin and Thereza leave the restaurant, sure they were going to continue the rest of their night naked. But, still, she couldn't shake the feeling that they were not together. He'd said as much at the bar, and for a split second, she had believed him. *What do you care?* she chided herself. Guys like him don't have girlfriends. They had side pieces, probably all models.

Nicole was huddled under her wool blanket when Destin came out of the alcove, three steaming bowls balanced in his arms. Delicious smells accompanied him. Her stomach howled when he placed a bowl and spoon in front of her. Magnus shot from the floor and dug in the second Destin placed the second bowl by his paws. Then Destin set his bowl down, went back to the kitchen and brought out two more plates, each holding half of a sandwich.

He placed one by her bowl, then slid into a chair across from her and gestured at the food with his spoon. "Bon appétit."

She shifted on the bench and dipped her spoon into the stew. She let out a small sound of pleasure and allowed the tastes to linger in her mouth before scooping up another bite. Her lips pursed to blow a cooling breath across the hot stew, and shifting her gaze, she caught him staring.

"This is good," she said after several spoonfuls.

"Yes, Lapin à la Cocotte. My grandmother's recipe."

She stiffened. "Um, this is rabbit?"

He tipped his head in answer, and she blanched. He snickered.

"I forgot. Americans only eat chicken," he said with a smirk.

Her eyes narrowed. "You're hilarious. I've had rabbit before. In Paris," she said defensively, leaving out that she hadn't finished the dish and ordered chicken. She continued eating, around the rabbit.

She raised her spoon and stared at the little square of

carrot submerged in brown broth, then let the liquid sit on her tongue again for a moment before swallowing.

"Tell me," he said.

"What?"

"The flavors."

She grinned, then closed her eyes in concentration. "Onion, butter, garlic, thyme, parsley, bay leaves, along with the carrot and potato, of course, bacon—although I don't see any chunks—and a hint of red wine."

"You missed one."

Her eyes widened, and she dipped her spoon again. Then again. She stared into space, took a drink of water and sipped the broth again.

"I can't believe this, but I taste nothing else."

A smile played on his lips, and a wicked gleam jumped into his eyes.

"Oh, you're screwing with me. Cute. Was that to get me to eat more rabbit?"

"I couldn't resist. You really don't like it?"

"I do like it. It's the thought of the cute fuzzy bunny that bothers me."

"The *bunnies* around here are not cute. They are wild vermin. And there is no bacon, only drippings used for flavor. Try the Bauru."

She took a big bite of the sandwich and let out a muffled happy squeal. Then finished it in about five seconds flat.

Destin finished his half quickly, too, except for a small bite he threw to the dog.

"Where in Paris did you have lapin?"

"Café Janou."

"In Le Marais."

"Yes." She smiled, surprised that he knew it.

"The chocolate pudding…" His eyebrows raised in appreciation.

"Oh, my God, yes. It's so decadent. I feel gluttonous

every time I eat it. You don't happen to have any back there in your magic kitchen, do you?"

"If only," he said with longing. "Tonight would be the perfect night to be decadent."

She searched his face, wondering if he was purposely trying to be suggestive. Maybe it was the way he was looking at her. Intense and interested.

He leaned in. "Do the sweets bother you?"

She looked away. Oh, he was interested…in her super palate.

"Only if too sweet." She pushed her plate away and adjusted her foot on the bench. "Thank you for lunch. I suppose I was lucky you were here. I'd probably be soaking wet and still looking for my car."

Destin took a sip of water and looked at her for a long moment. "Tell me more about what you do, Nicole." She liked his accent and how he said her name. Neecole.

"I help sell dreams." She smiled at his confused look. "Business and investment properties are my specialty. Developers, corporations and celebrities all want a property that will increase in value quickly, or won't lose value in a down market. This property, for instance, needs work, but the acreage, seclusion and ocean proximity make it very attractive. Property like this doesn't lose value."

"Interesting." The tone of his voice told her he didn't find it interesting at all. She reminded herself to be careful; she was selling his dream.

"Actually, it can be a lot of red tape. Hence law school." He grimaced, and she recalled his aversion to lawyers. "Do you plan on going back to Paris when the deal is closed?"

"I'm not sure what you mean."

"Oh, I thought you'd want to get back home with Elliot and your father."

"This is my home. I live in a small château fifteen minutes from here."

"I didn't realize you were still living here since..."

"It took a few years for the vines to start producing the amount we needed to open the business. My life has been here for almost eight years. Rio Grande is fierce and unpredictable, like today." He gestured toward the door. "But tomorrow she'll apologize with blue sky and warm winds. You'll be able to see the sunset over the mountains."

"Rio Grande is a she?"

"All high-maintenance entities are females."

"Excuse me?"

"It's true. Cars, boats, homes—all female."

Her eyes narrowed. "Because they are beautiful and mysterious."

"Because they are a lot of work." He smirked.

"Because they are more than you can handle, you mean."

He laughed out loud, which pleased her more than she cared to admit. "I certainly didn't do a good job of handling Rio Grande today." He jerked his chin toward her ankle. "Neither did you."

"No, I didn't."

"For the record, Rio Grande is a she because I worship her. She's provided many harvests for my family and is the mother to all we have planted. We were careless and destroyed the gifts she gave. My family and I no longer deserve her."

He lowered his gaze again and traced his fingertips over the table. The pause twisted her heart.

"You love her."

His lids lifted and he began a slow nod. "I love her."

"Destin, are you going to be able to let this go?" He stared at her. "This won't be yours in a month. You may be living next to a resort in a year."

"A month?" He blinked. "You're that good?"

"My buyers are pretty solid."

He didn't answer her question; instead, he fingered his water and glanced at the closed door of the cask room.

Destin cleared away the plates and strode to the kitchen, dropping the dishes into a large basin. He'd take them back to his château for a proper washing later, if they ever got out of there.

He heard her laughter and leaned over to see Magnus trying to lick her face. The sound was…sexy.

A sexy lawyer who was going to obliterate everything he owned in thirty days.

Gone in a month. His heart had almost stopped. He'd thought he'd have more time.

Destin washed his hands with some of the bottled water, patted his hands on his cargos and walked to the doorway. His breath caught when he saw Nicole standing—or rather, teetering—on one leg next to her bench.

"What are you doing?" He strode forward quickly, afraid she was about to tip over.

"I just wanted to see the room." He realized that the doorway to the cask room was open. Her head whipped around, and her eyes were wide. "Is there wine in there?"

"There is," he grunted as he stepped over her crumpled blanket on the floor. He hooked an arm around her slim waist and helped her settle back down onto the bench.

"You know, there are no medical supplies down here," he scolded her as he placed the blanket back on her shoulders and wrapped it around her body. "You need to be careful."

"I was fine until I put weight on my ankle."

"Yes, a sprained ankle."

She gave him an exasperated look, then murmured a

thank-you when he stepped back and took his place across from her at the table.

"I'll have to stay here and keep my eye on you."

"Too bad you didn't hook this place up with a TV."

"You've decided that talking with me has worn thin?"

"Not at all. I just don't think I've ever sat in one place for this long without being busy. Usually I'm doing paperwork."

"You don't know how to relax."

"Honestly, I don't think I do."

"Here. Watch me." Destin made a show of leaning his side on the table. Then he raised his brows in triumph. "See."

"Wow. Looks so natural," she said on a dry laugh.

"It takes practice."

"I'm sure," she teased. "You're the stereotypical glamorous vintner."

"Vintners are glamorous?"

"Of course, didn't you see *A Walk in the Clouds* with Keanu Reeves?"

"I did not, but I assume they didn't show the twenty-hour days picking grapes in the sun or the de-stemming by hand when the machine gets clogged."

"No. They showed the ladies stomping the grapes with their skirts raised."

"Ha-ha-ha. Of course. The part a vintner lives for. The stomping of the grapes is no longer a necessity. We have large shiny machines now, but it's a ritual we do before the autumn harvest. We use the ritual grapes for our house wine—wine only for the family."

"That's lovely."

"It's been our custom for five generations in France. My grandmother still stomps, but with my mother and wife gone, our female energy has dwindled to her, my aunts and a few cousins."

"Maybe if I can ever walk again, I can come and help."

His lids lowered. "I'd love to have you."

"Five generations is a lot of tradition."

"Tell me about it. It doesn't leave a lot of room for new ideas. Innovation is seen as destruction."

"You innovated and were successful, though."

"Yes."

"Is some of your success sitting in that cask room?"

His eyebrow popped up. *Don't trust her.* He was about to say no, give an excuse. Anything to keep her far from his plans.

She grinned at his hesitation, and his gaze focused on her lips. Decision made.

"You want a taste?"

Chapter 7

"Let it breathe a little. Then tell me what you think." Destin towered over her, waiting, watching, anticipating her party trick. At least they were getting along, she thought, her mind running over their unusual circumstances. Any mention of the sale had him closed off and frowning, but he was inviting when it came to his wines.

She reached for her goblet, giving the dark cherry-colored liquid a habitual swish before tipping it to her mouth. His gaze dropped to her lips, and she couldn't resist the urge to run her tongue over them. She wondered if he realized that he licked his own lips in answer.

The minute the wine hit her tongue, she splashed into heaven. Any echoes of awkwardness peeled away as her palate was bombarded with a full-bodied varietal infused with rich flavors. She tapped her tongue on the top of her mouth and sucked in a slow breath. Vanilla, coconut and sweet wood—probably from the light oak barrels she had seen in the other room. The dark undertones in the wine placed it as a Cab Franc, which made sense, since she had tasted something similar at dinner the night before.

But there was something different and more vibrant here. Could it be something in the aging process?

Destin shifted his weight and let out the breath he'd been holding, but his focus on her didn't waver. She took another sip, swished it around her mouth, tasting again with laser-sharp focus. A floral note teased her tongue, but the subtle flavor eluded her. Violet? She took another sip and shook her head. Basil? Her tongue swiped her lips. No.

"You're killing me," Destin grit out.

"Black currant, plum, black licorice, tobacco," she started.

The corner of his mouth lifted slightly, but his gaze told her there was more, as did her palate.

"Coconut, vanilla from the oak."

His brows raised in challenge.

"And a floral note in the finish that I'm still working out. This is a beautiful wine, Destin."

He didn't smile, but his face radiated satisfaction. "Thank you."

"So, was I right?"

He studied her and nodded slowly. "You have quite a gift."

"It's similar to the wine we had last night, but fuller. More explosive on the tongue."

His eyes snapped to hers. "You can tell the difference?"

"Absolutely. This one is crisper. Your father's wine had heavier wood and earth flavors."

"It was one of the first wines I created and produced."

"Oh! I thought that was your father's."

"It is his." She caught the change of tone in his voice. "Technically." Destin walked back into the cask room.

Half a glass later, Nicole was surprisingly baffled and

impressed at the complexity of the wine. A wine like this would sell for hundreds of dollars a bottle.

Nicole bet all of those casks were filled with wines created before the fire, and she estimated that many would be mature. If she was right—and she usually was—there was about two thousand bottles' worth of wine in there that could be sold in a year and used as capital to fix the irrigation pipes and replant. So why wouldn't they rebuild?

It wasn't her concern. She was there to show, sell and get her promotion. Not save a dilapidated winery or its even more dilapidated owner. He clearly hadn't moved on, and how could he when everything in here probably reminded him of a lost life? Destin probably didn't realize it, but the sale would be good for him.

A streak of satisfaction caused her to sit up a bit, and she recalled their meeting last night. He'd called lawyers "soulless." She'd taken offense, of course, but mostly because it was true. While she tried to use her degree for good, there was a downside to her occupation that she had to ignore in order to be successful. Development deals were always at the expense of long-time residents; many home sales were executed because of financial trouble.

There were times she felt she made money off other people's pain. But this was different. This deal made her feel like Mother Theresa. The Dechamps family healing was in her hands. Not to mention this deal, and the promise of a new life that would be her path to healing, too.

"I'm going to finish up in here," Destin said, reappearing behind her. He grabbed the wine bottle and refilled her glass. Then his own. "I have some books in the back if you'd like to try to relax." He winked. She was pretty sure she blushed in return.

Her gaze followed him back to the alcove and fell to his tight-fitting cargo pants. His whole body looked solid.

Horrified at her thoughts, she tore her gaze away and took another sip of wine—the culprit of her wandering thoughts, no doubt. She needed to slow down, but the wine was so good.

She could see a shadowed outline of him bent over as he rummaged through something in the darkness of the alcove. Then he lit an oil lamp, and he was bathed in an ethereal glow. She couldn't look away.

As if called, the dog popped up from his rest, plucked a rawhide bone from the floor and sat by his master. With a smile, Destin turned and ripped the bone from the dog's mouth for a small toss. In seconds, the dog had retrieved it and was waiting patiently with his toy in his mouth for another go. After a few throws, Destin turned, sipped his wine and went back to his project.

Undeterred, the dog made his way to her side. His soulful eyes looked into hers, and she got sucked into playing fetch. With each pitch to the dog, Nicole suspected that Destin wasn't cleaning, as he'd claimed.

"Good boy, Magnus. Go lie down." When the dog didn't budge, Destin repeated himself in Portuguese. The dog lowered himself just a few steps away. "Magnus isn't very worldly. He only speaks Portuguese."

"I won't hold it against him."

"And if you haven't noticed, he's quite clingy. I suspect he is part sheepdog. Herding is instinctual, so he gets antsy when we move around."

"That's kind of cute."

Destin held up two books. "By chance, are you an Oscar Wilde fan? It's in English."

A scorched leather-bound copy of *The Picture of Dorian Gray* was balanced in his fingertips, bringing the fire to the forefront of her mind. She saw now that the covered furniture, the food, maybe even the dog, were all items he had pulled from the rubble. She wondered how this book had survived. She wondered how Destin had survived.

"Or Steinbeck? *Of Mice and Men*? Although this copy is in French. I have more, but they're in Portuguese." He paused. "They were my wife's."

She nodded. Maybe that explained why he couldn't let go.

"Dorian Gray it is."

She had no idea how much time went by as she sat and read while Magnus worked on his rawhide nearby. She twisted around toward the closed cask-room door where Destin had gone.

It occurred to her that she hadn't heard any storm sounds in a while. It had been hours; the storm had to have stopped.

The dog set down his bone and watched as she carefully lowered her ankle to the floor, whipped off the blanket and stood. She limped to the door and pulled it open. A muffled thunder crack filled the stairwell, and she could hear the rain pelting against the wooden door above.

Hopes dashed, she closed the door, and the dog seemed to lead her back to her spot at the table. She bundled up and sipped her wine, wondering if Gustavo had called the hotel to check on her. She'd been supposed to call him after finishing her tour.

She thought of Dani and Liz, and wondered what they were doing. Her best friends were probably at brunch getting tipsy on mimosas, scanning for men and trading gossip. She wanted to be there so badly. She couldn't wait to tell them about this.

Nicole drained her wine, feeling cozy and a little floaty, and...oh, no. She hoped wine cellars had toilets.

She knocked on the cask-room door and shouted, "Um...is there a bathroom?" She already knew the answer, expecting some sort of bucket situation. He cracked the door just enough so his body was visible, and his eyes told her what she already knew.

"There's an outhouse about fifty yards from here."

"It's still storming. I can't hobble out there."

"I could find a bucket—"

"Absolutely not," she said, horrified. Her dignity was already holding on by a thread. It wasn't the 1600s, where chamber pots were the norm.

"Then you'll have to wait out the storm."

She affected a pleading look and a sweet smile. "Are you sure we can't take my car out of here? It's an SUV with four-wheel drive."

"You want me to carry you out to your car in the storm, then drive us down the washed-out roads where there are no guardrails or any guarantee that the roads are clear of fallen trees?" He looked away and bent behind the door, then set an old ceramic plant pot down next to her. Her jaw dropped at the same time that he shut the door.

She let out a sigh and began to chew on the inside of her cheek, not only to distract herself from the increasing urge to relieve herself, but to think of some serious insults to hurl his way.

Ignoring the pain in her ankle and hopping furiously, her movements so aggravated that the dog whimpered, she made it to the door and whipped it open. The bang it made against the wall echoed. The rush of rain only spurred her on; she wasn't going to let Mother Nature or that arrogant Frenchman best her.

She made it to the first step and let out a loud yelp when strong arms grabbed her, twisted her around and pulled her into a hard chest. His breath was hot against her ear, and his beard brushed her lips when she moved to grasp his shoulders. With her nose in his throat, she inhaled him, and was surprised by a natural, spicy scent of forest and firewood.

He set her down at the top of the stairs and opened the outer door to a torrential down pour.

"Here is what we are going to do!" he yelled over the rain. "I am going to go get my Jeep." He grasped her arms and brought his face to hers, eyes wide. "Do. Not. Move." Magnus gruffed at her side, as if to accentuate the order. "I'm going to pull up to the door, help you in, and I will do my best not to get us killed on the way to my home. Got it?"

She nodded and shivered as the wind blew rain against them. She was getting spritzed, and she could tell by the darkening stain on his shoulders that his whole back was soaked.

Magnus followed Destin out into the night, and she cursed under her breath when she could no longer see them. The rainfall coming from the dark sky was relentless. Scattered lightning flashed lavender in the distance. Without the barrier of his body, she, too, was wet to the bone. Ironically, she no longer had to pee.

It felt like it took forever, but suddenly two headlights and what looked like an army Jeep stopped just a few feet from her. Rain pelted Nicole's eyes, but she saw Destin jump from the vehicle and come toward her. Suddenly she was in his arms, moving quickly to the other side of the Jeep. He placed her inside roughly and slammed the door.

She jumped when Magnus licked her shoulder from the backseat. Outside, Destin secured the cellar door, then jumped into the driver's seat. He was breathing heavily, his wet hair spiked, his shirt sucked tight across his torso and bulging arms. The open V at his neckline gaped, and the skin there glistened. It was the sexiest thing she'd ever seen.

"Ready?" He turned to her, his gaze dropping to her shirt, which had been made completely see-through by the rain. She didn't care; a part of her wanted him to look. He turned away and clicked the hot air on high. The warm blast helped her find her voice.

"Yeah. Ready."

Chapter 8

Even at the slow pace Destin was driving, they fishtailed out of the forest and onto the soupy roads. The wipers were set on high, but Nicole could see nothing except for what was right in front of them—mud splash and rainfall. Her seat belt cut into her torso as they bounced hard over fallen tree branches, and Destin's jaw clenched as he handled the steering wheel.

They skidded and swerved, Destin's arm going out across her body. She felt them turn, then trees thumped against the sides of the Jeep as they drove. Branches pelted the side of the car as a large gate rose before them.

Destin flipped his key fob up and pressed hard, but nothing happened. "Shit. The electricity is out. Stay here."

Jumping from the Jeep, Destin crossed in front of the headlights and pulled at the gate, manually sliding it to the side. He jumped back into the Jeep and they bounced and dipped along an unpaved lane that led into a gated community.

Destin whipped the Jeep into a right turn and stopped just in front of a dark structure. He hurried around the car and helped her to the front door.

"We made it," he said, fiddling with his wet keys.

"Thank God," she breathed, her skin so wet the warm wind made her shiver when she climbed out of the car. "Not to sound ungrateful, but I left my purse in the cellar."

"We'll get it tomorrow. I locked it up. Hang on to me."

She clutched his shoulder and hopped over the dark threshold. Even with the door still open, it was difficult to see inside.

"Stay here. I need to find my flashlight." She stood in what she thought was a foyer, shaking from the chill of her wet clothes, willing her eyes to adjust. Magnus breathed rapidly beside her, his wet fur against her leg a comfort. She hated the dark.

Banging, shuffling and a muttered curse came from different parts of the room. She squinted in each direction. Destin had become a hulking figure moving away into the dark. Rain continuously pelted the roof and the windows. Lightning flashed through a giant bay window on the other side of the room, and for a second she glimpsed a kitchen to her right and a wide-open living room right in front of her. But where was Destin?

"Destin?" Could this get any creepier? She felt Magnus shake his fur out and move away. She tensed even more. A door opened. "Where did you go?" Her question was directed into the darkness.

"I'm right here. I…" he said, suddenly only a few feet away from her. He didn't get a chance to finish as Nicole let out a scream that had Magnus barking. She heard a match strike. Destin's face and form became illuminated by a skinny white candle. "Sorry," he said with a smile that looked more mischievous than apologetic.

Behind him was a spacious kitchen with a rectangular

island, dual ovens, a microwave, a refrigerator and the largest wine locker she'd ever seen.

She placed her hand over her heart, willing it to slow. "I think I'm about to have a heart attack. I, uh, I don't like the dark."

"I see." Chuckling, he handed her the lit candle and laid several more unlit ones on the counter. "I must have left the flashlight in the wine cellar. I found these."

He pulled mason jars from a cupboard, placed a candle in each one, and then turned to Nicole. "Can you make it to the couch?"

Candle in hand, Nicole hopped to the middle of the room and, instead of sitting, provided a beacon of light while Destin strategically placed candles in each dark corner. The glow of each candle revealed more of what she had glimpsed in the lightning flash: a large open family area with tan leather armchairs and a beige L-shaped couch, a corner sitting area by a small liquor bar and bookshelves, and a small dining table right under the bay window. What he called a small château was more like a sprawling estate, and could have graced the cover of *House Beautiful*.

"Where's Magnus?" Nicole asked, scanning the hardwood floor covered strategically in luxurious, fluffy rugs.

"Probably on his bed in the other room."

Nicole leaned on Destin as they crossed into an adjacent room with storage shelving. Magnus was lying on a flat pillow. He dropped a toy from his mouth and stood when they entered. Two pairs of rain boots were against the wall next to a side door.

"A mud room," Nicole said as she noticed the concrete floors. "How many rooms do you have?"

"You're not selling this, too, Nicole." The light played on his jaw and cheek. Too sexy.

"I'm just asking. And you never know," she said as they

turned back into the living area. "You may want a change. I could get you a ridiculous price for this."

He grunted his disapproval. "Enough of the tour. We have to get out of these wet clothes."

They managed to make it to his bedroom. The candle exposed a massive oak bed and a single chair covered in clothing. A floor-to-ceiling window with French doors took up most of the east wall.

Nicole gasped when lightning streaked across the sky, illuminating things again. "Is that a terrace?"

"Yes," came his muffled voice from a walk-in closet. He emerged with a pile of clothing. "There are stone stairs that lead to the ocean. I'll show you in the morning. But you won't be able to use the stairs with that ankle."

"You could just carry me," she teased.

The look he gave her said he wasn't amused. "Aren't we here so you can use the bathroom?"

"You haven't shown me the ladies' room."

"Follow me." She limped after him down the candlelit hall to the guest bathroom. He set the pile in his hands on the corner stool. "I don't have any women's clothes. But you can change into these and leave your clothes here to dry. Then feel free to make yourself comfortable in the living room."

"Thank you." He nodded and turned to leave. "Destin. Really. Thank you."

His eyes looked navy in the firelight. "You're welcome."

She set her candle on the sink and closed the door, thankful for a proper toilet. She hopped to the stool and sifted through the clothing. A large black terrycloth robe, a large T-shirt, a pair of soft pants and thick socks. Sexy.

She sat on the stool and changed, taking her time, opening the window to let just a bit of the air into the humid space. Everything was way too big for her, the T-shirt falling over her nakedness like a minidress, but the clothes were warm and dry. The pants were so long she needed to roll them, but the fabric wouldn't stay. With her bad ankle, she could see herself tripping or worse.

Leaving the pants on the stool next to the rest of her clothing, she slipped on the socks, then tied the robe tightly around her waist. The overlap concealed her legs, and as long as she sat like a lady, no one would know she wasn't wearing underwear.

Last but not least, she limped to the mirror above the sink and cringed at her stringy hair. There was no helping it.

Emerging from the bathroom, Nicole followed the flickering glow from the candles around the room and found Destin by the tan leather ottoman opening a bottle of wine. He was in a gray T-shirt and the same type of soft pants she'd left in the bathroom. His bare feet were planted in the soft rug. It was almost…romantic. The only things missing were music and a charcuterie platter.

"Do I look homeless?"

He chuckled when he saw her and continued pouring two glasses of wine. "You look adorable. Come, get off that ankle."

Nicole made herself comfortable on the plush couch, clenching the robe together at the knees, and took the wine glass he offered. She was fully covered. Honestly, she looked like a bear, but the fact that her panties were drying in the bathroom made her hyperaware of the way she was sitting.

She took a calming sip from her glass. "This is your father's Cab Franc. The one from dinner."

"It's truly remarkable that you can tell the difference," he said softly, walking from the candlelight into the shadows. Cupboard doors began to slam and utensils clinked.

"You said something like that earlier," she said, her voice carrying into the kitchen. "Why does it surprise you so much?" Magnus ambled into the room and stretched out at her feet. She reached down to rub his belly. When she came up, Destin was setting a large wooden block of bite-sized food on the ottoman.

Pitted olives, pickles, cheese triangles and a small mountain of prosciutto lay in front of her. "These will spoil if we don't eat them now. I'm sorry, it's not much. I seem to be out of everything," Destin said, popping an olive into his mouth and settling into a lounging position on the other side of the couch.

He smiled then, one arm stretched across the back of the couch while the other hand balanced his wine glass on his knee. *The Prince in repose*, she thought.

"And to answer your question, my father argued that the signature wine from Dechamps Brazil—the one featured in *Wine Spectator*—was too close to his signature wine, and therefore he took my wine and slapped the Dechamp France label on it."

Nicole frowned. "That's illegal."

"Not if you were dumb enough to sign a contract stating that any wines created on Dechamp lands belonged to the parent company."

Nicole frowned. "Why would you sign that?"

Destin lowered his gaze. "I trusted my father and his team of lawyers." Nicole had the decency to blush. "It didn't matter that I created both signature wines, my rights were gone the minute I put my name on that contract." Destin drew deeply from his glass and topped it off, then leaned over to refill hers, as well.

"Both of the wines? No wonder you hate lawyers." And it explained why he was fighting with his father. "Sounds like working with family isn't all it's cracked up to be."

He grinned. "Think about all of the annoying things your boss does that affect you, then imagine that man is your father."

"Hmm, no. That doesn't work."

"Exactly. There is security in family, but every dinner or holiday ends in a business discussion. There is no separation of church and state."

"Wow. I never thought of it that way."

"But don't get me wrong. We have our good moments." His gaze hit the rug. "I love my family. Very much." An awkward pause descended. "Do you have siblings?"

"No," she said, shaking her head.

"Children?"

"No," she said, unsure she wanted to discuss such personal details.

"A boyfriend? Or husband?"

She shook her head in answer.

"Why?" Instantly his gaze softened, which made her uncomfortable.

"There's no reason. I focused on my career. And I'm proud of that." She heard the edge in her voice and instantly regretted it. "Actually, I'm up for a promotion."

His lips formed a flat line, and his gaze didn't waver from her. "I'm sorry. I didn't mean to strike a nerve."

"No, it's just that I won't allow anyone to hold me to a stereotype. I haven't met the man of my dreams. Not everyone can have it all." It was her turn to trace patterns on the table. The adoption agency came to the forefront of her mind. She might not have it all, but she was going to get damn close.

She squirmed, preferring him in the hot seat. "Are you and Elliot fighting about the sale?"

"You don't want a family?"

They spoke in unison, each apologizing politely for interrupting. Destin gave her the floor.

"Are you and Elliot fighting about the sale?"

"No. Elliot is a lot like our mother was. He hovers. He meddles. But it's always with a good heart." He paused. "We aren't fighting, but he gets himself caught in the middle when our father and I do fight."

"And you and your father are fighting now."

He lowered his eyes and slowly nodded. "Your turn."

"I did want a family. Sure."

"You did," he repeated. "But no longer?"

She sighed. "I still want one, but time isn't on my side."

"What do you mean?"

"I mean I don't have the luxury of waiting for a man."

"Because of your age."

It wasn't a question, but rather a statement. It stung. She felt her walls go up and the bolts slam into place. "I don't think this is something you discuss with strangers."

"Not even strangers who saved your life?"

She snorted. "My life wasn't in danger."

"Those shoes tried to kill you. You could have fallen down the stairs. Or broken your ankle or your wrist trying to catch yourself. You don't know what tragedy was prevented because I was there. What do they say in the kung fu movies? Your life is mine, now."

The corners of her mouth lifted. "Spoken like a true Shaolin master. You like kung fu movies?"

"Elliot was obsessed with them when he was little. I had to chaperone him because our parents refused to go. They were dubbed in English and subtitled in French. Awful."

She laughed, happy to change the subject. "I used to watch them at a friend's after school."

So many nights she had come home from junior high and, while her father was passed out, done her homework, made dinner, then gone to her friend's apartment across the hall. It was a time she never thought about if she could help it, but never forgot.

"Is your family in New York, too?"

"My parents passed away some time ago."

"I'm sorry."

"Thank you." She knew what he was thinking. No husband, no children, no family. She drained her glass and made methodical work of the food.

Destin wondered if he had gone too far, but he'd been surprised at the fact that she had no one at home waiting for her. She was intelligent, accomplished and—he watched her lips close around a small pickle—sensual. It was obvious in the way she savored her wine, the curve of her lips when she smiled and in the foods she chose to eat. Maybe she was as selective with men as she was with her palate. Or maybe she hadn't found a man who could stimulate all of her senses.

She was wrapped in his robe, reclining against the couch arm, her legs stretched out and crossed at the ankles. He watched as she eased forward and reached for another olive. The slippery sucker eluded her, and she stretched farther, keeping a tight grip on the terrycloth over her legs.

His breath caught when she lost the handful of fabric and the robe fell open to expose her leg from foot to thigh. She quickly covered herself, forgetting the olive to grab a slice of prosciutto, and sat back primly. He had a rampant urge to drop to his knees and trail her inner thighs with kisses. The thought had him adjusting his seat and also thinking he should have worn less flimsy pants.

"So, what's wrong with you?" He hadn't meant the question to be so direct, but he was still getting a hold on his libido.

"Excuse me?" One eyebrow went up.

"Why don't you have a boyfriend?"

"Wha…well… I don't know… I date. Things just don't always work out."

"You have a list of requirements, don't you?"

She cocked her head. "Everyone has a list."

"Men don't have lists."

"Yes, they do. Hot? Check. Boobs? Check. That's a list."

"And how many items are on your list?"

"I don't know…a few." Her gaze dropped to the floor. More than a few, he'd bet.

"I would venture that you, Miss Parks, are a control freak."

Nicole sat up straighter. "No, I just know what I want. I think that makes it easier for everyone involved."

"What you want is not always what you need."

"Whoa, is this more kung fu wisdom?"

"No, that's my mother."

She took a deep breath. "I'm sure your mother was right. She sounds very wise."

"She was. She was independent, like yourself. I think she would have liked you."

"Really? She didn't hate lawyers?"

Destin's lips twitched. "I should clear something up from last night. You are not the first attorney we've hired. The others were all hotshot men who thought more about lining their pockets than what was best for us or Rio Grande. None of them worked out. My shock wasn't because I'm a chauvinist. I just wasn't expecting…" he paused "…you."

She smiled, and when she spoke again, it was in a teasing tone. "But you are a bit of a misogynist."

"No, I just tell bad jokes. Elliot is the people person in our family."

"So, how is working with a female lawyer so far, Destin?"

It took him a moment, but he leveled his gaze on her. "Jury is still out."

Chapter 9

Nicole tossed and turned in the night, assailed by a list of things that had to be done the next day and concerned that the storm would never cease and would turn the property into a giant mud pit. Her buyers were powerful—and impatient. At this rate, it could take days for the place to dry out, which meant delayed showings and the risk of lost interest.

Sinking into the pillows, she mused that the pitch black of the unfamiliar room was making her feel like time was slipping away. How dare Destin ask such personal questions? She didn't need him making her feel like a failure at love; she did that all on her own. Nicole used to say she was alone, not lonely, but somewhere along the way it had turned into straight-up lonely. A family of her own would vanquish that feeling, hence her wanting that promotion. Yes, she deserved it, but as fabulous as her single life had been, she was ready for more.

Everything would be different after she became a

mother, wouldn't it? No longer would she feel that hole in her heart, the one that she wasn't able to fill, ever since the people who'd loved her disappeared. Often she wondered if her friends were right, that she was barreling head-on into adoption without thinking it through. But she had thought about it ever since the pregnancy scare she'd had with her last boyfriend.

She'd found her NuvaRing on the shower floor and freaked, remembering their late-night water playdate, where they'd both wanted to get dirty before getting clean. Staring at the contraceptive device, she'd counted back to her last period and felt…joy. A little fear and uncertainty were present, of course, but there had been happiness, too.

Her boyfriend? He hadn't felt the same way.

A lawyer himself, he'd said all of the right things that you say to a woman when she might be pregnant. Supportive phrases that Nicole had suspected he didn't feel. He'd bought the drugstore test and tried to seem unconcerned, even as he questioned whether she'd removed the ring herself. And, when the test came back negative, he'd slumped, relieved and smiling, against the kitchen counter. Nicole had wanted to cry.

Not long after, he'd pulled away, blaming the demise of their relationship on her job. She'd lost hope for romantic love, but her desire for a baby, a little family all her own, still lingered.

Destin's blue gaze wafted through her thoughts. He wouldn't be like that. From the way he'd taken care of her that night, it was obvious he had parental instincts. Maybe he'd even wanted to become a father, before his loss, of course. He'd turned somber when she spoke of the deaths in her family, but there was something else in his eyes, something Nicole recognized in her own. Loneliness.

Unable to fall back asleep, Nicole thrust the covers aside and placed her feet firmly on the floor. A quick splash of water on her face might quiet her active thoughts. She moved to find her candle and matches, the darkness of the room and its frequent purple illumination from the lightning unnerving.

Lit candle in hand, she crept forward out of the bedroom doorway, favoring her still-tender ankle, listening hard, unused to the eerie silence of the unfamiliar home. She preferred to hear taxicabs whizzing by on the streets below, or a verbal fight happening on the corner. Not this Edgar Allen Poe-like quiet where her heartbeat thumped in her ears. She turned her attention in the direction of Destin's closed door, but again heard nothing. Did he sleep nude? She'd seen his bed, but what did he look like in it?

Remembering her nakedness under the long T-shirt, she scurried to the bathroom and quietly shut the door. Placing her candle on the sink, she ran the water and made use of the facilities, grateful for the cool breeze from the window she had cracked earlier.

A movement caught her eye, but a quick inspection of the shower stall, Jacuzzi tub, sink and closed door calmed her. "Just your own shadow," she murmured at her reflection in the wall mirror. Leaning toward the stool, she fingered her clothes, which were laid out and slowly drying.

Quickly, she pulled her hand back from her lace panties, blinking a few times, unsure if the candlelight was playing tricks on her. Surely the flickering was what was causing this dark…thing. The thing moved.

Nicole's loud yelp bounced off the walls, and her rigid body knocked the mason jar that held her candle into the sink. Pure black enveloped her. She couldn't breathe. She couldn't move. Magnus's barking sounded instantly outside the door.

"Nicole!" Destin's voice and heavy footfall traveled up the hall. She heard her name again, along with several knocks. Then the door burst open. Destin's eyes were wide and glittered turquoise from the lit candle in his hand. He was shirtless, in only his loose trousers, and Nicole was momentarily distracted by the picture he presented in the doorway.

With the shadows behind him, he looked larger than life—all smooth skin, rippling muscle and chiseled torso. Her gaze caught on the light smattering of dark hair on his chest, hair that also covered his forearms and, starting below his navel, disappeared below his thin cotton pants toward the bulging outline of his...

She snapped her gaze upward.

"What happened?" His distressed gaze traveled over her in seconds and landed back on her stricken face. "Nicole, what's the matter?"

Unable to find her breath, she rapidly shook her head and pointed. A fuzzy black tarantula, the size of a child's palm, sat unmoving on Nicole's pink underwear. *Thank God*, Destin thought. The ugly but harmless creature was more of an annoyance than a threat. Destin frowned at the crack in the window, apparently the creature's entrance. The scary intruder had been looking for shelter and found it on pink lace. Good choice.

"It's okay. It won't hurt you." Destin said, doing his best not to ogle her. His T-shirt fell to the tops of her thighs, and her unbound breasts quivered against the thin fabric. Those long legs were naked, exposed and gorgeous. And unless she'd had another pair of underwear with her, her panties were underneath the spider. Blood from his brain rushed straight to his lower body.

"It's huge!" Nicole backed against the wall.

His gaze flicked to her face, which reflected terror. He supposed she'd never seen anything like it in person. He didn't want to tell her he'd seen larger ones just outside the winery. "Come out so I can remove it."

"They can jump!"

"No, that's the movies." Actually, they could, but they didn't usually jump at creatures larger than themselves. Destin came toward her, shielding her view.

"Lean on me and let's get to the hallway." She was skittish as a kitten, and her nails dug into his biceps when his arm came around her waist for support. Her eyes never left the spider, as if willing it to stay. Magnus shuffled in and, with a curious bark, sniffed at the insect. The spider began to back away toward the wall.

"Uh...uh...it's moving!" Nicole jumped on one leg out the door, unaware that her T-shirt fluttered up, giving Destin a glimpse of her smooth bare ass. His mouth went dry, and he ran a rough hand through his hair.

Destin set his candle down, kicked Magnus out of the bathroom and grabbed the fallen mason jar from the sink. In one swift motion, he trapped the spider against the wall and watched him fall into the jar. *Sorry, little guy*, Destin thought as he shook the spider out into the rain, which seemed to be letting up, and shut the window tight.

Nicole was leaning against the wall facing him, her T-shirt riding up slightly as she hugged herself. The hem of that shirt beckoned, and he prayed a gust of wind would come suddenly from the floor. But he felt bad when he saw her face.

"It's gone. You're okay. Everything is okay," he said gently, alarmed at her unraveling. The events of the day must have finally been too much to handle. Her features shifted from afraid to wary to calm—though it seemed fake.

"I don't like spiders," she explained in an embarrassed tone, her gaze darting past him to scan the bathroom. She bit her bottom lip, and he felt his blood slow.

"It's gone," he whispered again, reaching for her shoulder to comfort her. He sucked in a breath when she pushed herself against his chest. Her hands found his back, and she held him in a tight hug. He held her close, feeling her body relax. It felt lush against him, her curves so supple.

He should back away. The soft pants he wore couldn't hide what he was thinking, what she was doing to him.

"Thank you," she whispered, turning her face up to his.

His gaze dropped to her mouth, and when she didn't move, all he could think of was tasting her. Their gazes locked in the dimly lit hallway. One breath went by, then another.

Stroking the backs of his fingers over her cheek, he held her chin in place as he leaned down and brushed his lips over hers in a featherlight kiss. The brief contact had them gripping each other harder, their ragged breaths mingling as they reached desperately for each other. On a shaky breath, she slid on tiptoe, reaching for him with lips parted. He cupped the back of her head, holding it in place.

The lights in the hallway went on. Inches from each other's lips, they stilled, seeing each other as if for the first time. Somehow, the darkness had made them simply a man and a woman, but the light smacked him over the head with who she was and what she was doing there. He couldn't do it.

"Nicole," he breathed, abruptly sliding his hands away. "My apologies. I didn't mean to—"

"No, this wasn't...we shouldn't..." she said, quickly tugging her shirt down. Her head tipped to the side and her eyes seemed to focus on anything but him. It cut him deep, especially since his body was still reacting to their kiss and the feel of her in his arms. All he wanted to do was touch her again, while she seemed annoyed and uncomfortable.

Of course she's uncomfortable, Destin scolded himself. *She's trapped with a stranger, and you're semihard.*

"I would never take advantage of you," he blurted out. "That's not what this was."

"I know," she whispered, her arms going around herself again. "Good night, Destin."

She hurried into the bedroom, and he stood there staring at the door long after she'd closed it.

The next morning Destin took the stone steps to the beach, Magnus on his tail, and watched the sun rise over the ocean. The pink-and-yellow sky changed to blue, and the sun was hot on his face. Leaves blew languidly, and the waves churned against the shore. Except for a few fallen tree branches and dampness on the ground, it was as if it had never stormed.

With Nicole and the previous night heavy on his mind, he threw himself into the ocean, slicing through the water in a smooth breaststroke, stopping only to take furtive glances up to his patio. She hadn't stirred since she'd closed the door on him. The longer she slept, the more time he had to figure out how to face her. What to say? *I'm sorry I tried to make love to you last night?* If he was honest, he was sorry he hadn't.

The minute he woke, her lips had bombarded his thoughts, and he'd angrily set out to exhaust himself in the warm sea. With each stroke, he hoped to rid himself of the images that still burned in his brain. The warm curves of her body, the satin of her skin, the velvet of her mouth in the darkness. Thinking about it felt like a dream. The stroke of her palm on his face, her fingertip over his chest. And with new light after the storm had come the pain of reality. But damn, being there in her arms had felt so good.

But that was last night. The morning had brought a new day, one where she was an obstacle to his plan to fight for his land. Getting rid of her and ruining this deal was supposed to have been easy. And it still could be, if he didn't get a heavy dose of guilt and anger just thinking about hurting her. What should he do? He stopped pushing himself and trod water, looking to the sky for answers.

A sharp bark in the distance pulled him from his carousel of thoughts. Destin continued treading water and watched Magnus trot back up the stairs.

She was awake. Nicole was on the patio, peering out into the sky. Then she tipped her head and dropped her gaze to him.

Her hair was in a ponytail high on her head, and she was still in his T-shirt—probably still naked underneath. He felt his pulse accelerate even more than it already had. With each stroke back to the shore, Destin steeled himself. He hadn't planned on the unavoidable intimacy that was now between them, but it wasn't going to keep him from his primary objective: his land. She was a smart, capable person, and when this deal fell through, she would go back to New York and work on another deal. Simple.

He toweled himself off and climbed the stairs back to his bedroom. The sound of running water came from the guest bathroom. It must be spider free, he thought with a chuckle. Images of their kiss surfaced, but he shook them off. He took his shower and dressed in a light T-shirt and jeans, coming to a conclusion once he felt awake, clean and fortified.

Last night was just a misunderstanding, a product of their circumstances. Yes, he might be feeling some attraction, but he was a man, and she was a very, very beautiful woman. It didn't mean they were soul mates. It didn't mean anything. He fed Magnus and found his Jeep keys on the table. In fact, it was best that he drive her straight to her hotel, drop her off and never see her again.

The guest bathroom door opened, and steam rose into the air. Nicole emerged, wrapped in a towel from her breasts to her upper thighs, her skin damp and glistening, her hair still high on her head. With her clothes in her arms, she quickly limped her way to the bedroom and quietly shut the door.

He needed to take another lap in the ocean.

Destin aggressively searched his cupboards for anything resembling breakfast. He had an egg—one egg, and it probably needed to be thrown out. He had enough ground coffee to produce about half a cup, no bread and they'd finished the rest of the food from last night.

"Good morning," Destin heard behind him. He slammed the cupboards closed and whipped around. Nicole slid into a barstool and leaned her elbows on the island, looking fresh-faced and cheerful in her rumpled silk blouse. The movie in his mind replayed her legs locking around him, and his fist clenched against the feeling of her breasts against his chest. He wondered if they should talk about it.

She straightened her back. "Look, I don't want to talk about last night."

He blew out the breath he'd been holding. "Okay."

"It's not that I regret it or anything. I just think we got… caught up."

"Caught up?"

"In the moment," she continued quickly, seeming to have a hard time looking him in the eye. "I was hysterical. You were my knight in shining armor."

"I was in lounge pants." He didn't know why, but he was offended by her cavalier attitude. He'd almost had her, and if that damn electric company hadn't finally decided to do its job, he'd still have her in bed.

"You know what I mean," she said, finally looking at him. She sounded nonchalant, but her eyes held a pleading look. As if asking him not to make her admit that she'd wanted him, too.

"Yeah. Caught up. No worries." Destin gave her a quick nod and grabbed his car keys. "Should we go?"

They stuck to pleasantries after that. He asked after her ankle, noticing she could manage a slow limp. While she put on her heeless shoes, he double-checked that all the candles were out in the rooms. She'd made her bed perfectly, he noted, poking his head into the guest room, and had left the towels spread out over the desk chair to dry.

He was walking back to the living room when he saw Nicole shove at a bit of pink lace that was peeking from her skirt pocket.

Destin ran a hand over his mouth, unable to get the glimpse of her naked ass out of his head.

Yep, he *really* needed to take another dunk in the ocean.

Chapter 10

They made the short drive back to the property in silence, with Magnus panting happily in the backseat. Destin parked by Nicole's car at the front gate. The rented SUV was covered in dirt and leaves, but seemed unharmed.

"Stay here. I'll be right back," Destin said, opening the door and unfolding himself from the Jeep.

"I need my purse!" Nicole shouted from the window.

"I'll get it for you."

"But I want to walk the property again. I need to see what I'm selling."

The word made Destin want to hit something, and he raised his voice. "You can't walk, Nicole!"

"I'll be fine!"

They both swallowed when they realized they were yelling.

"Fine," Destin said calmly. "Just let me survey the property before you go in." Nicole looked like she was about to protest, but his face told her not to go there. She didn't.

Destin walked across the property and found himself inside the broken structure of his old home, palming the cool stone of the former kitchen. Everything looked in place. Even the ground wasn't too soggy, the sun and the surrounding vegetation strong enough to suck up the excess water.

Quickly, he walked behind the cellar and stomped through the dense trees until he came to the clearing where his small crop of vines now thrived. Going down the rows, he spot-checked the leaves, tested the firmness of the grapes and checked the gravel base around the trunks of the vines for proper drainage. They seemed fine, and he smiled at their resilience—against last night's storm and the fire.

But he wasn't sure he could protect them from Nicole.

The forest was thick enough that no one suspected anything was back there except wild animals, but that was no guarantee that the tenacious real estate lawyer wouldn't stumble upon them.

And then she'd tell his father.

And then he'd lose them.

He wasn't going to let that happen, regardless of what had happened between them the night before. What he was going to do was get her out of there and make sure she never came back.

After a quick trip into the celler, he was relieved when he found her sitting in his Jeep, right where he'd left her. He opened her door, handed her her purse and helped her slide to the ground. With him behind her, Nicole limped as fast as she could to the middle of the property and stopped when she hit open ground. She tipped her face to the sky and let out a loud sigh of relief. She looked at Magnus, who'd kept pace with her the whole way. "It's like the storm never happened. Is it really already this hot?"

She was standing very still, eyeing the sky, the trees,

the land. She twisted around slowly, stopping to look toward the acres of burned vines in the distance. "You said the irrigation pipes were ruined. Right?"

"Yes," he said with a lump in the pit of his stomach, afraid of where her questions would take them.

"And what's back here, behind the cellar?"

"Just forest," he said in a low voice, praying she wouldn't go over there.

Sure enough, she stepped forward, carefully skirting the rocks and fallen debris. Rustling in the far trees above caught their attention, and she stalled. Movement and a small face showed through the leaves.

"What is that?" she breathed.

"It's a monkey," he answered, debating whether or not to tell her it was harmless.

"Oh, God," she whispered, limping away. He chuckled and threw a silent thanks to the little animal, then followed her.

"Nicole," he said to her back as she limped across the grass ahead of him toward the front gates. Afraid her pace would make her stumble, he caught up to her. "They are harmless and rarely make an appearance." She wasn't listening. "And they only eat leaves and shoots. Slow down. You'll hurt yourself again."

He should help her, but the images of the night before were at the forefront of his head. He didn't need any more touching. No more talking. No more helping.

She stumbled and was in his arms in a second, protesting in his ear, but she became resigned when he refused to put her down. He tried to think of her as a sack of grapes, or potatoes, or something inanimate that didn't make his blood pulse.

With Magnus on their heels, they made their way through the small patch of forest and ended up at her

SUV. She slid from his arms and practically hugged the car, wiping off the leaves and grime with her bare hands.

"Thank God the car is okay. I can drive to the hotel and grab a much-needed nap." She plopped her purse on the hood of the car and rummaged for her keys.

"Nicole, is that your driving foot?" Her face told him it was. "Give me your keys."

"Destin. I *need* to leave here."

"We are leaving. But I'm driving. Keys."

Destin helped her inside, and then let Magus hop in the back before he walked around the car and slid into the driver's seat. After securing his seatbelt, he looked up and caught Nicole's gaze on him, but she looked away quickly and plugged her phone into the dashboard charger.

"Seatbelt," he said.

"Air conditioning," she replied as she clicked in.

He held back a smile. The engine roared and he pulled out into the road, slowly taking in the damage. Destin navigated mud and chunks of rock, potholes filled with water and midsized branches. They were half a mile down the road when a man in a construction hat flagged them down. Behind the worker, a group of men with chainsaws and MCats were cutting into a fallen tree blocking the road.

Destin lowered his window and spoke briefly with the man, then turned to Nicole. "We have to go the other way. He says it's clear, but traffic is bad." Destin executed a three-point turn and proceeded back the way they'd come.

"What time is it?" Nicole asked. Although the car seemed to be working fine, the instrument panel on her rental was wavy as if water logged. Looking up, he spied a small crack in the sunroof that was the culprit. Her phone showed a white screen as it updated itself while his was in his pocket.

Leaning toward his own window, he looked up and found the sun. "My guess is it's around eight."

"Did you just check the sun?"

"I'm a vintner. I wouldn't be much of a good one if I didn't know the weather or the angle of the sun during the day."

"That's kind of impressive," she said, her voice still a bit throaty from the morning. His body responded, and he gripped the wheel for concentration. "But we have no clocks to see if you're right."

"I'll fish my phone from my pocket when we get on smoother roads, but I'm right." He felt a small triumph when she remained silent. "When is your appointment?"

"It was supposed to be this afternoon. A casino owner from Texas—little restraint and lots of money. I wouldn't be surprised if he brought his bid in cash in a bag in the trunk of his car. If he got a flight in, that is. I wish I could check my messages."

Destin frowned. "He wants to build a casino? Here in Porto Alegre?"

"You'd be surprised how much money these things generate."

"The people who live around here don't have money." Destin tried to control his tone, which was dangerously close to an edge.

"No, but tourists do. Tourists with yachts."

Incredulous, he looked at her.

"It will bring jobs to the community, Destin. And he is prepared to give back. Taxes, obviously, and donations. He's talking about setting up a free shuttle from the hotels."

"This is not a good idea."

"Your father vetted my clients and was pleased."

"Of course he was," he murmured in disgust. "I want to see that list."

"I don't have it right now," she said, pointing at her phone. "You can get it from Elliot."

"A casino is not what we need."

"What does the city need?"

"A business that won't rob its community!" Instantly frustrated at himself for raising his voice, he calmed down and stared past her, as if the roof of his home was visible through the trees. "Excuse me if I don't want to live next to a madhouse."

"You're being dramatic," she said softly. "Didn't you say you didn't want to be involved? That might be for the best."

Destin's voice was low and unyielding. "I want to see that list."

She sighed. "I have a hard copy at the hotel."

They drove in silence for most of the way. Nicole took in the gorgeous terrain on the other side of the mountain, while Destin's mind raced with ways to make sure a casino never opened its doors in Rio Grande. He'd been wrong about her. She was just as cutthroat as those other lawyers, maybe more so, since she hid it so well. He'd have to step up his game. Make sure that her list of interested clients dwindled to nothing. Then he would happily pay for her ticket back to New York.

He slid another glance at her. She leaned forward and studied something out the window, taking an interest in her surroundings. So she could better sell it, no doubt. She let out a gasp. "Look!" A waterfall was cascaded over the rock of a deep canyon. Nicole turned, and her animated face and smile took his breath away.

He wanted to kiss her. Hard. So her iron will would bend. So she'd forget why she was here and see his point of view. So she'd let him make love to her.

Ridiculous. "It's a watering hole. Locals swim there." Destin gripped the wheel and turned back to the road.

As they got closer to the heart of town, concrete buildings, graffiti murals and teens on motorbikes streaked past. Traffic began to congest, and finally they stopped completely as horns honked around them and cars jostled for leverage. They were fifteen minutes from the hotel, but at this rate, they'd be there in an hour.

He was starving, which didn't help his already foul mood. His mind flipped through different paths to take to her hotel, but he had a feeling they were all jammed. He decided to take a chance. If he was going to be with Nicole for more than an hour, he needed sustenance.

Destin twisted his body and made a gesture at the car next to them.

"What are you doing?" Nicole asked.

Destin didn't answer. Instead, he worked the SUV to the side, through the traffic, amid honks and angry yells. Once out of the fray, he proceeded down a small alley and onto a dirt road.

"Wait, the hotel is that way."

"I know where it is."

"Look, I know you're upset about my buyers, but I was brought here to do a job and—"

Destin drove up to a one-story ranch house that sat on miles of flat rocky land. Then he threw the car into Park and got out without explanation. A line of people stood off to the side, and a few more were at benches in an outside seating area.

"What are you doing?" she yelled from her seat as Destin walked to her door. She raised an eyebrow at him when he opened it.

"Are you hungry?"

"A little," she said without looking at him. He'd bet she was starving.

"You can yell at me inside. Let's go." He held out his hand, and she slipped her fingers into his as she gingerly lowered herself onto her good foot.

"I'm not yelling," she said sheepishly. Destin whistled,

and the dog squirmed from the backseat to the front and jumped to the ground.

"Hmph. Can you walk?"

"Yes." Her eyes flashed with defiance.

"Good." He shut the car door and kept a close eye on her slow gait as they made their way up to the small porch.

"How are you going to show the property when you can barely walk? You should cancel."

"My ankle is better. It's just that these shoes aren't really flats. And you should mind your business."

"Rio Grande is my business." He pulled his phone from his pocket. "And it's 8:20." With that, Destin strolled into the establishment ahead of her.

Chapter 11

Fuming, she stared at his back as he entered the restaurant, watching his athletic stride. She didn't have the strength to argue with him, not after a sleepless night. That kiss. What on earth had she been thinking? She hadn't been, only feeling.

The adrenaline pumping through her body had been from more than that stupid spider. Destin had looked like a god in the doorway of the bathroom. All skin and muscle, with tossed bed hair and that wild look in his eyes. When his arms had come around her, she'd never felt safer. It was a moment she'd wanted to capture forever; maybe that was why she'd reached for his kiss.

It had been the briefest of touches, but his mouth had fit hers perfectly. When she'd reached her bed, she'd thrown herself under the covers, praying the humiliation she felt over his pulling away first would knock her out cold. But the minute she'd closed her eyes, she could feel his lips on hers again and his hands trailing her skin.

Had she even slept? She remembered the sun rising, along with the realization that it was the next morning. She'd lain in bed feeling embarrassed, a little angry and sexually frustrated. The shower hadn't helped. Her empty stomach didn't help. Seeing him swimming, with his skin glistening in the sun, hadn't effing helped.

She'd made the decision then—she wasn't going to think about it. And they definitely weren't going to talk about it.

Destin propped the door open, waiting only a few seconds to watch her slow approach before turning his back and continuing inside. Fine with her. She didn't need his help. She couldn't wait to be relieved of his presence. Just a little bit longer, and then she could forget about him... and that kiss.

The smell of coffee and food made her mouth water, and she limped through the inside of the little restaurant, which wasn't much except dark wood and square tables, but the backyard was spectacular. Picnic tables graced with wildflowers and tea lights were set up in the grass. Fragrant citronella torches peppered the area, and tall poles were anchors for strings of tiny lights that were on, even in daytime.

Nicole saw Destin shaking hands with an older man, who then bent to give Magnus a pat on the head. The man rushed forward at the sight of Nicole, helping her to the table while speaking rapid Portuguese. Nicole smiled and nodded.

"Ela é Americana," Destin told him.

"Oh! Welcome, miss. Please enjoy." Their host waved at a server. "Destin and I have been friends a long time. The wines are—" he kissed the air "—superb. Please Destin, more soon. Yes?"

Destin shifted uncomfortably, nodding curtly and flashing the man a look.

"Okay." The man smiled and was off to another table.

"What was he talking about?" Nicole asked.

"Nothing." Destin shifted his attention to the server, who, Nicole noticed, was young, beautiful and wearing only a bikini top and shorts. She was like the Brazilian version of Aaliyah. Her breasts threatened to spill out of her swimsuit top as she bent and poured them both water.

"Café?" Aaliyah asked with a lazy drawl. At their enthusiastic nods, she pulled menus from under her arm and walked away.

Nicole must have made a face because Destin gave a low chuckle. "It's a surf community." Destin grinned. "Jimmy Choos don't matter here."

"Nor do tops, it seems."

"Nor underwear." Her eyes widened. "Why did you put yours in your pocket?"

"I don't know what that tiny monster was doing to them. Laying eggs?"

"Ridiculous," he said with a smug look.

Their gazes locked in a silent battle of wills. They were hungry, dirty and moody, but for all of the tension between them, all she could think about was that kiss. That kiss. Would she ever forget the feel of his hands on her body?

His shoulders looked broader in the T-shirt, and his hair had been finger brushed into perfection. She looked away, taking in her surroundings, and focused on what she did best.

"Maybe we should ask your friend what he thinks about a casino being here. I'm sure he would appreciate the tourist business."

Destin's eyes narrowed. "Do you see that line?" He pointed to the string of people she'd seen when they first pulled up. "Most of them are off to work on the small farms in this area or the next town, which is more than an hour away. Others are doing odd jobs in town or in the favela. They aren't poker players or card dealers. Half of them wouldn't pass for a job as a bouncer or whatever casinos need as security."

"People can be trained."

"This isn't Las Vegas."

"It's not?" Nicole's voice rose, and she feigned surprise. "Between the bikini tops and the heat, I couldn't tell."

The coffee arrived, along with whole milk and a basket of rolls with butter and jam. Nicole took a sip of her java and stilled. She had never tasted a cup so fresh or crisp.

"Why is this the best coffee I've ever tasted?"

"It's probably local," he said, reaching for a roll. "Organic. Possibly picked days ago. Brazil is one of the largest producers of coffee in the world."

"Do you drink this type of coffee every day?"

"Mmm-hmm. Tomorrow there will be a market in town, and everyone will be buying coffee, grains, whatever they need."

"It's a weekly market?"

Destin nodded, tapping his coffee cup. "At the square. Hopefully, you won't be bringing in a Starbucks to take a look at Dechamps."

Nicole stared at Destin for a moment and decided to ignore him. She held up her menu, grateful it was translated into English, but she noticed the selection was scarce— small meat plates, smoothies, fruit and bread.

"Breakfast isn't a main meal in Brazil. You won't find eggs on the menu, but I can have him make some."

She half expected to see annoyance in his face, but his eyes held genuine concern. "There is ham, cheese, a plate of fruit and couscous."

"What's couscous?"

"Like cornmeal. Steamed."

They settled on the ham and fruit, with a plate of scrambled eggs for Nicole.

She needed to calm down. His opinion of her buyers and her job shouldn't matter. She didn't work for him; she worked for his father, who didn't seem to care about… what was best for the people of the town.

She sighed inwardly. Was Destin right? Was she only thinking about herself and her promotion? Things change, or they don't survive. Destin was still holding onto a fantasy that had died years ago. There needed to be new opportunities for these people. She could provide that.

"Nicole. I—"

They were interrupted by a flurry of plates and food. More coffee was poured, and another bottle of water appeared on the table. Whatever Destin had been about to say was forgotten.

They had utensils, but the ham was rolled into small logs, the papaya and mango were halved, not sliced, and the rolls were perfect for tearing. Except for the eggs, it was a meal they could eat with their hands. It was relaxing and kind of fun.

Afterward, Destin helped her back into the SUV. In seconds he'd slid inside and started the engine.

"We should be back at the hotel in an hour. Not bad— traffic should be better," he said, turning on the air conditioning.

"Thank you for breakfast. That was way better than sitting in traffic. It's a cute restaurant."

"It is. Preserving places like this is important to this community," he said, pulling onto the road that led back to the town. "And now I'm going to show you why."

Destin punched the accelerator on the SUV, and with the traffic cleared, they found themselves in the city within minutes. White and gray skyscrapers, boutiques and cafés whizzed by. The working class hurried on foot to their jobs amid armed police officers. Destin rounded a corner and slowed. They were on a tree-lined residential block with seventy-foot-high trees that twisted into the sky and created a regal green archway. Shade blanketed the car, and it felt like they were entering another dimension.

"What in the world?" she said in awe. The trunks were thick and majestic, and Nicole imagined local kids trying to climb and play among them.

"These are Tipuana trees. They've grown here for over eighty-five years. Ten years ago this whole area was threatened with a mall development. The people protested for months. Now it's a cultural site preserved by the government."

She turned and met his gaze, aware of the not-so-subtle message. "That's a lovely story."

"A true story. The people protect their quality of life here."

"Are we ever going to get to the hotel?"

"Sick of me already?"

"We're way past that." Nicole grinned.

They picked up speed and drove through the metropolitan area as he pointed out a beautiful park with a lake and small, romantic bridges. Not far from there, both the art museum and the grand theater were a mix of old and modern architecture with fountains and inviting white steps.

A massive silver dome rose in front of them, and Destin's eyes lit up. "May I introduce Estadio Beria-Rio, our soccer stadium? We call it The Giant."

"I can see why." The building stretched for several blocks, with white flags billowing all around the exterior.

"It seats fifty thousand people and was built with cement and brick donated by fans." His pride was obvious, and his message was more and more clear. "The body of water next to it is Guaíba Lake, a perfect place to watch the sunset," he continued. Nicole saw kids playing along its banks and lovers strolling hand in hand.

As they moved on, Nicole could tell they were getting

closer to the sea. The air smelled of salt, and she felt the heavy wind when she cracked a window to get a better whiff.

Destin slowed again as they came upon the public *mercado* in the town square. Pounds upon pounds of ripe produce, meats, seafood and textile goods sat in a canopied two-story building that covered several blocks. Although it was still early morning, the place teemed with local customers.

They sped along the pier, with Destin explaining the early morning fish auctions and the best fish restaurants in the city. Before she could ask a question, they were in an alley and stopped at a dead end. It looked as if a small mountain of grass and sand had swallowed the road.

Destin was out of the car and walking toward the dune; Nicole hurried to follow. Magnus ran full speed ahead and vanished, but his barks could be heard in the distance. She smelled the ocean the minute her feet touched the ground. Ahead was a wooden bridge, and they followed its gentle swell to the vast expanse of a gorgeous beach. Seagulls cried, the wind whipped their clothes and the sun gave no mercy as it bounced off the crystal water.

Nicole forgot Destin, her disheveled state and the pain in her ankle as she kicked off her shoes and limped toward the ocean. She was a city kid, so beaches were like the eighth wonder of the world to her. Nothing was man made, buildings didn't block the sky and the sun virtually kissed you. She marveled at how the ocean carved out its space and was a home to creatures she knew little about.

Nearby, Magnus played a game of splash with the tide. It was still early, but a few umbrellas spotted the miles-long shore. She bet the place would be packed with families and laughter in a few hours. Water washed over her toes, and she walked in farther, covering her bad ankle, letting the ocean heal it. Would she go to the beach with her daughter one day? The sea foamed and splashed at her calves, and she took that as a yes.

"You look like you're about to dive in." Destin was at her back; their shadows touched.

"I'm not a strong swimmer, but I like the beach," she said over her shoulder.

"Do you see this place?" he said, his lips at her ear. "There is no boardwalk, no carnival, no—"

She whipped around. "I get it. No greedy corporate developers who will ruin your way of life. I understand. But things can't stay the same forever. And just because it's new doesn't mean it's wrong. I'm not here to tear down your life."

His hair whipped in the breeze, and he lifted his gaze over her head to stare out into the sea. A loud caw from a seagull was too close, and they both bent as a shadow passed overhead. Nicole looked around to make sure the coast was clear, then grimaced when she felt something wet on her shoulder.

"No. No! I can't take it!" She cringed, her body stiffening in disgust.

"What?" He frowned and came around to stand in front of her.

She pointed and then he saw it. The white-and-brown slime of bird poop. The harsh lines of Destin's face softened, and his deep laughter cut through the wind. She wanted to curl up into a ball in the shower and cry, but when she saw Destin bend down then rise with a broad smile and a little seashell, she began to laugh. Her dignity had left her hours ago.

"What is that going to do?" she said, grimacing.

"It's a scoop. For the poop," he joked, but then he proceeded to scrape the goo from her blouse, still chuckling. She refused to watch, feeling humiliated, not just by the bird but by all the theatrics of the night before. "I hate you," she said with a small chuckle.

"I didn't do this to you." He was so close she could smell his shampoo.

"No? I think you paid that bird. That's a trained actor bird."

The warmth of his laughter brushed her ear. "It's good luck, you know."

"Yeah, I feel incredibly lucky."

She could feel him smirking as he finished. He stepped away and tossed the little shell. "All clean."

"Not even close," Nicole said with a sigh. "We need to leave."

"We are. Back to your hotel. Come."

Her feet had sunk into the wet sand, and Destin held onto her hands, helping her forward. She stepped close to him and smiled up into his face. His gaze slid to her mouth and lingered for a moment. Then he stepped forward and slid his hand around the back of her head. Before she knew what was happening, his head lowered, and he kissed her.

A shock wave of heat burned through her.

His mouth moved over hers in a slow, thorough exploration, as if taking what he couldn't the night before. She rose on her toes, gripped the back of his head and kissed him back. She had no rationale for her reaction; she wanted him. It was that simple.

Heart pounding, she opened her mouth in invitation. Her hand moved from his nape to his cheek, and she rubbed the stubble at his jaw, loving how rough it was over his smooth skin. He jerked, and she was afraid he'd pull away. Instead, he captured her tongue in a sensual duel and pulled her closer. His hand slid down her back and plundered her mouth, as if he needed her taste to survive.

All around them, the ocean lapped at the sand and the sea blended into the sky, but nothing else mattered except the pulsing of her body and the relentless beating of their hearts. The night before hadn't prepared her for this raw display of sexual need. He was kissing her, touching her. The steel she felt at her stomach was for her, and it was sizable.

The last thought had her insides melting. She wondered what it would take to break down every barrier he'd ever built.

His grip on her body loosened, and before he could push her away, she eased out of his grip and stepped back. Chests heaving, they stared at each other. Her head spun, and by the blurred look in Destin's eyes, he was also very affected by what had just happened.

What *had* just happened?

"I'm sorry," he breathed in the wind.

He'd said that last night, too. "Sorry for what? Kissing me or pulling away?"

"Maybe both," he said, half grinning. "You..." He searched for a word. "Affect me. But things are complicated. You aren't here for long, and I'm not looking for anything real."

"I'm not offering you anything real. But if you wanted to spend some time together while I was here, I'd spend it with you."

He looked at her a long time, his gaze shifting out to the sea. "It's time to go," he said. He waited for her to pass by before falling in step behind her.

As the SUV barreled through the city, Destin's face and body language were closed, making Nicole feel stupid for offering to "spend time" with him. She might as well have just whipped her skirt over her head.

Truth be told, she ached to touch him. She slid her gaze to her stone-faced driver, not caring if he noticed her staring. Damn, he was handsome.

But he'd rejected her. Again. And as if the last twenty-four hours hadn't been complicated enough, he probably thought she was completely unprofessional.

He didn't trust her, which was why he was tentative about sharing the rift between him and his father. Why couldn't he see that she was there to help?

The puzzle pieces of the man next to her were floating in her head when he slowed and stopped in front of her hotel. She was about to say goodbye when he climbed out, as well, and handed the keys to a valet. Oh, right, they were in her rental. She made sure she had her phone and bag, then climbed out.

The SUV pulled away, and they both stood there on the street, staring at each other. Magnus came to her legs and sat.

"Here you are," Destin said, glancing up at the hotel. "In plenty of time for the casino guy." She heard the sneer in his voice.

"Will you and Magnus be there, scowling at my buyers?"

A smile tugged at his lips. "Unfortunately, no. We have other plans. How are you getting there? I don't want you driving with that ankle."

His possessive tone wasn't lost on Nicole, and it gave her a boost of hope that he wasn't just dumping her on the street before ghosting.

"They will be meeting me here, and we'll take their limo up."

He gave a satisfied nod and let his gaze linger on her face before falling to the ground.

"Am I going to see you again?"

After a deep inhale, he sighed. "I don't know." She knew what that meant. It was a cop-out. He wasn't going to make an effort. Well, then, neither was she.

"Do you want to know how it goes today?" They'd have

to exchange numbers for that. And if one of them sent a dirty text later by accident, so be it.

"I won't be around."

Right, no texts. She might never see him again, and the thought made her hesitate. She wanted to say something and tried to meet his gaze, but he was scanning the area. "Fine. Thank you for…an adventure. Take care." Irritated, she turned and gingerly walked into the lobby, trying not to feel like she'd just been dumped. Their kiss kept flashing in her mind. That son of a bitch!

Air-conditioning cooled her skin, and she caught a glimpse of herself in the hanging mirror. It looked like she'd died, was resurrected, then turned into a zombie. She recognized Anton's tall frame behind the counter, and his light eyes went wide with relief when she appeared. He began to shout orders she couldn't decipher, and the staff immediately presented her with a wheelchair.

Anton helped her sit. "We're very happy that you are well, Miss Parks."

"Thank you."

"And you, Destin. Are you all right?"

Nicole whipped around. Destin had followed her? He didn't meet her gaze. Magnus came over to inspect the wheelchair, pushing his nose into her hand.

"I'm fine, Anton," he said with a firm handshake. "Call the doctor for her. On my tab."

"At once. And for you?"

Destin shook his head. "I just wanted to make sure she was being taken care of. On second thought, you can call me a car."

"Consider it done. Anything else?"

Destin's gaze slid to hers, his blue gaze intense.

Her heart sped up. Whether they liked it or not, there was something between them, and by the look in his eye, he knew it too.

"No. Nothing else."

Her heart sank as she was wheeled away into the elevator.

His brow furrowed and he lowered his gaze, then the doors closed.

Chapter 12

Nicole saw the stretch limousine pull up to the front of the hotel and hurried through the lobby doors to the sidewalk. She didn't feel at her best, but something else was nagging at her. She couldn't shake Destin's talk of bringing in businesses that wouldn't benefit the town, and as she stared at the shiny black luxury vehicle, she was afraid that he might be right.

Clay "Junior" Winchester pulled his six-foot-five, three-hundred-and-fifty-pound frame ungracefully from his stretch limo, shifted the white Stetson on his head and showed a big Texas smile.

"Well, hey there, little lady. Good to see ya again."

Nicole carefully walked forward in black jeans, a light blazer and Converse sneakers. The painkillers and the compression sock the doctor had prescribed were working wonders. Clay was in his jeans and signature cowboy boots, making Nicole feel less underdressed. She shook his hand, ignoring the *little lady* comment. Clay was a good ole boy from Dallas, where they called everyone "little."

"How was your flight, Clay?" While Nicole's morning had been filled with rescheduling all of her other appointments due to last night's airport closure, Clay had fired up the private jet and voilà.

"Just fine. Slept the whole way. Right here is my CFO and my real estate consultant, Chuck and Diane," he said, gesturing to the fully suited man and woman who followed him out of the car with laptops and briefcases.

Nicole extended her hand to both, then addressed all three. "Welcome to Porto Alegre. I know we planned to go straight to the property, but if you need to eat or rest, there is time."

"Hell, no." Clay slapped his thigh. "Let's see this place."

Twenty minutes of easy driving later, they were all standing in front of Dechamps.

"Don't look like much." Clay frowned, his hat brushing low-hanging branches. "I thought it was gonna be bigger."

"We're outside the property gate, Clay. But don't worry, it's big. I know you Texans like big."

"You're damn right."

"Well, how about you follow me, and we'll see if I delivered." Nicole's gaze dropped to Diane's high heels. "You need to be extra careful. I lost my Jimmy Choos in there."

"Oh, my Lord," Diane said, horrified, and rightly so—she was wearing classic black Christian Louboutins.

Clay's phone went off. Instead of answering it, he handed it to Chuck. "I don't want to talk to my daddy right now." Chuck forwarded the call to voice mail.

A rustling in the trees had them all whipping their heads around.

"What was that?" Clay asked, seeming more thrilled than scared.

No one moved or answered until the sound was gone.

"Are there animals in there?" Diane asked, her voice cracking.

"Nonsense. It's just some frogs and such. Right, Nicole?" Clay asked.

"Right, yeah." She shrugged and nodded. "Or a monkey." Three pairs of eyes stared at her. "But they keep to themselves."

"I wanna see a monkey! Can you imagine me coming home with a monkey?" Clay scanned the trees.

"I doubt you could get it past airport security," Nicole said, noticing Chuck's eye roll.

"Chuck, find out what I have to do to get a monkey around here." Chuck nodded with practiced patience.

And this is what Nicole loved and hated about Clay. As the baby of the Winchester family—who had owned the Winchester arms company for fifteen generations— no one had ever said no to him. Ever. The only defeat he'd experienced was when he had been kicked out of South Africa when the government found out he was trying to make a real-life Jurassic Park. Genetic research and everything. Just like the movie.

Now casinos were his hobby, and much easier to get approved.

"Maybe I should stay in the car," Diane said with a grimace.

"Woman, I told you to wear your boots, but you didn't listen. Chuck has his boots on."

Nicole gave Diane a sympathetic tip of her head. "You'll be okay. There's a cleared-out path through there." Nicole pointed into the foliage. They frowned. "It's just around this gate." She pushed at a few oversized plants, showing them the path.

"This trail needs a lawnmower," Clay said behind her.

"You can probably widen it with a machete," Nicole stated.

"A machete? Chuck! Find me a machete when we get back to the hotel. I don't feel right without my gun."

It was Nicole's turn to roll her eyes.

They made a single file through the greenery and safely made it out into the clearing. The sun couldn't have given the property a better day to show itself off. Nicole almost expected to see Destin—wished, was more like it—but there was no sign of him.

Clay stomped through the rubble of Destin's crumbled home. "Oh, yeah. I like this. Look at that burnt-down house. That could be a real haunted house, ya know, for Halloween. Just like our driver said." Clay turned to Chuck. "Maybe we should keep it."

"Back up," Nicole interrupted. "Your driver said what?"

"He said this place was haunted by the souls of all the workers who died here." Clay's voice trailed off in a dramatic whisper.

"Seriously?" Nicole frowned.

"Yep, he said no one in town goes up here. But that will change once I build the best casino in the country."

No one had told her anything about haunted souls. "Well, it wasn't a ton of workers who died here. It was the owner's wife." Saying it made Nicole's heart ache.

Clay frowned. "That's terrible. Chuck, should we keep the house for Halloween?"

Chuck's sigh was audible. "Your building plans were not approved for a Halloween house."

"Hmm, I guess it will have to go. What's this doorway over here?"

Nicole's throat tightened when Clay started toward the wine cellar. Just as she was about to follow, three dark-skinned men in khaki jumpsuits came out of the forest.

One of the men carried a metal box, and they all had

strange tools hanging from their belts. Nicole thought they looked like ghostbusters. The one with glasses stepped forward. His hand went up, and he addressed the group in Portuguese, then in English. "Stop. Go no further."

"Olá," Nicole said with a quick wave. "I'm a real estate broker here on behalf of the Dechamps family. They are selling this land and—"

"No, that's not possible," the man said, adjusting his glasses, which looked too big for his face. "I am Dr. Lima, and these are my associates. We are government land inspectors." He pointed to a patch on his right shoulder that looked like an official badge of some sort. "And we are deeming this place uninhabitable."

"Uninha-what?" Clay shouted.

Nicole straightened. "As a representative of the Dechamps family, I have the proper permits to sell this land, which was deemed habitable and saleable by their private inspectors several weeks ago." Nicole pulled out the notarized and stamped paperwork she carried along with her ID and held it up. "And since when does the government have the authority to inspect land when it's privately owned?"

"When the lives of the people and its surrounding habitat are endangered. Our research shows that this mountain is due for an earthquake." One of the associates held up the box, which was a digital seismograph. The numbers counted down wildly. "In five days."

Nicole stared at the counter, then her gaze slid to the doctor, who was sweating around the temples. She didn't have the paperwork on her, but the detailed inspection information she had read never mentioned any threats of natural disasters—which made sense, since there were no volcanoes or fault lines in the area. She stepped up and addressed the leader.

"That's very strange, Dr. Lima, because, as I'm sure

you know, this area has never experienced an earthquake. All of the seismic activity that Brazil encounters is on the Pacific side of the country, along the border of Peru, to be exact, approximately thirty-one hundred miles away." The doctor blinked several times. Nicole continued. "May I see some identification?"

Suddenly the counter went wild, and the three inspectors pulled a strange tool from their belt and began walking in circles where they stood.

"What the hell is going on? Look, I'm Clay Winchester, Junior, of the Dallas Winchesters. And—"

"Did you feel that?" the associate with the box whispered.

"What?" Clay asked.

"A tremor."

Diane mumbled nervously to Chuck. Nicole didn't feel anything. She pulled out her phone and tapped on her MyShake app, the earthquake detector app that she and her colleagues used to conduct superficial inspections. Other than the steps of the "inspectors" in front of her, the app detected nothing.

She turned to Clay. "There's no tremor here."

"What is that?" Clay asked.

She held up her phone so the inspectors could see the face. "Earthquake detector. No tremors."

"Holy hell!" Clay whipped around. "Chuck!"

Chuck had Clay's phone in his hand. "Already on it."

"That can't be accurate," said Dr. Lima. "And we have more work to do, so I suggest you leave."

"We aren't leaving." Nicole hadn't worked in Brazil in the past, but she knew that seizing privately owned land for no reason was against the law. These men were trespassing.

Dr. Lima straightened. "Miss Parks, I will call the authorities if I have to."

Nicole went silent, her gaze landing on the closed door of the wine cellar.

Clay stepped up. "Look, that's not necessary. Nicole, I've seen enough. This place is as big as three football fields, from my expert estimations. And a good jump away from the town." He touched the brim of his hat with a finger. "That's just what we're lookin' for. But if these guys are right, I don't think we can move forward."

Nicole gave Clay a solemn nod, her thoughts pinging in all different directions.

Clay led the way back toward the gates. Nicole was stepping onto the exit path when the realization hit. She had never given the "inspectors" her last name. "I'll be right there," she called to the group in front of her before turning back toward the clearing.

"Hello?" she called into the foliage. She was sure that was where they'd gone. She stepped high over the bushes and lumbered forward, ducking under trees and thick leaves. "Excuse me!" she called again. Where could they have gone?

Stomping forward, Nicole realized the foliage had thinned, and suddenly she was staring at rows of yellow-tipped plants. Then she saw a thick vine nestled inside the yellow blossoms, gnarled, dark and strapped to a short wooden pole—an older vine, she suspected. The base of the vine was covered in gravel, for drainage, probably, especially in the wet climate. The green leaves were healthy and protected the ripening grapes that hung under them. A long white tarp lay discarded a few feet away.

She scanned for more vines and found them scattered across the small field, each with a yellow flowered companion, or what she now suspected was mustard—a natural crop cover that helped control viruses in the soil. The raw edges of the small field told her that machines had no part in this. Had Destin handpicked vines from the wreckage and replanted them here?

"Nicole?" She heard the echo of her name on the wind. Her heart jumped, hoping to see Destin. Instead, Clay's hat and pudgy face appeared through the trees.

"I'm coming!" she yelled back, afraid he'd find her, feeling suddenly protective of the hidden crop.

He shouldn't have done that, Destin thought, watching with binoculars from the edge of the property as Nicole and the casino owners took their leave. They'd rushed the plan when Anton had given him a heads-up about her showing that day, but Rui, or should he say, Dr. Lima, had pulled it off. The big one with the hat looked thoroughly confused. And by the look on Nicole's face, *angry* was an understatement.

If the casino company representatives were anything like previously interested buyers who had come up against a surprise during their showing, they'd be on the next plane back to America that afternoon. Destin was satisfied that the stunt had bought him some more time, but the thought of hurting Nicole in any way left a bitter taste in his mouth. Especially when the taste he craved was her.

Chapter 13

Sunday morning, Elliot met Nicole for breakfast in the hotel. He looked up from his salmon hash, a specialty not on the menu, and patted Nicole's hand as she explained how the inspectors ruined her showing.

"I know of no such inspection unless Destin authorized it, of course. Which I highly doubt."

"Well, someone spoke to them. They knew my name."

Elliot's gaze softened, then focused on Anton as he brought them fresh-squeezed orange juice. "Don't worry about this. I will look into it. And if you see them there again, call me immediately."

"Of course."

Elliot glanced at his watch. "How did it go, otherwise?"

"I know Clay wants to make an offer, but he's going do his own inspection now."

"As he should," Elliot said with a slow nod. "But I'm not concerned."

"But it may delay an offer. And I need the keys to that

cellar. Clients will want to see the inside. The only reason Clay didn't was because we were kicked off the property." Elliot's agitated nod made Nicole feel like she was asking too much, but full access to all doors on the property was necessary for her to do her job.

"You're right. I'll get you a set."

"And what are these rumors of a haunting?" she asked. Anton again appeared, pouring them water.

"Ah, yes. Anton, you remember the haunting stories, don't you?" The two men exchanged knowing looks, then Elliot continued. "The local community believes spirits live on the land. It's a vicious rumor that won't die. It's also part of the reason we had to seek outside buyers. Superstition is very powerful here." Elliot sipped his coffee. "Anton, do you remember who started those rumors?"

"Children," Anton said and shrugged.

"Oh, yes, kids," Elliot said snidely, his gaze lingering on Anton's face.

Nicole was definitely missing something.

They finished their meal, and Elliot encouraged her to sightsee the rest of the day. He rose and kissed her on both cheeks. "I will investigate and report back. And I will call you about the keys." Nicole saw Elliot glance at Anton before he left the restaurant. She twisted around to thank Anton, but suddenly he was nowhere to be found.

Taking Elliot's advice, Nicole left the hotel in search of the weekend *feira*, or street fair. It was a beautiful day to explore, something Nicole would have done sooner had she not been stuck on a mountain for twenty-four hours. With her little language book in hand, Nicole found the locals that she stopped for directions friendly and informative.

Soon she came upon rows of wooden stalls set up with beautiful striped tablecloths, all in the brightest colors, and a variety of fruits, vegetables, cheeses and meats were meticulously displayed in massive amounts. Spices, coffee and savory, slow-cooked dishes teased her nose, and an array of colorful dried beans in plastic bags were flying off the tables.

Nicole strolled slowly through the crowds, her senses bombarded and her limp forgotten, thanks to the painkillers. She bought a *pastel*—a light, fluffy square of fried dough filled with cheese, tomatoes and oregano—then she purchased a dozen more with different fillings and tried to remember why she'd ever given up cheese.

In the next booth, an older woman and her young daughters sold handmade dresses and scarves. Nicole fingered the fabrics as they waved in the breeze, thinking it would be nice to replace her ruined skirt and heels with something more weather appropriate. The relentless humidity made her tank top and cotton shorts feel like burlap.

The silky scarf she caressed felt cool in comparison, and she wondered if Destin had turned on his misty cooling system. *Stop it, Nicole.* She walked on and found a wall of familiar brown wool blankets. Visions of him flashed in her mind.

Maybe she wasn't his type. She pictured him with a young, thin, natural beauty, like in those Herbal Essences commercials—women looking fresh faced in leather sandals and strappy dresses, kind of like the red floral one that was in her hand. She held it up.

"I'll take this one." Nicole let the girls style her. She left the stall with two dresses and a pair of sandals.

She was biting into a fruit-filled *pastel* when she spotted broad shoulders and well-fitting cargo pants moving through the crowd. Destin. Even though his back was to her, there was no doubt it was him. Magnus was happily by his side, taking his time to lift his leg and mark a pole or two.

Her feet sped up as if on autopilot. Maybe he knew

something about that strange inspection? She did need the key to the cellar. Yes, that was a good reason to be chasing him down the street.

Through the throng of people she saw him slow and— *what the hell?* Her jaw dropped when a honey-skinned woman with gorgeous dark hair ran up to Destin. Her smile was broad and welcoming, and when her arms came up, Destin stepped inside them without hesitation. Even the dog's tail wagged rapidly.

Herbal Essences. She knew it. Well, she thought as she moved closer and half hid behind one of the vendor booths, he *did* have a girlfriend. She bit her cheek, hard. A stunning young—Nicole frowned as a tall dark-skinned man joined the couple and threw his arm around the young woman. Nicole saw his face and stilled. He wore no glasses or overalls this time, only a T-shirt and jeans. But Nicole recognized him instantly.

Then she saw Destin count out a large amount of money and hand it to the man. They were friends? No, it couldn't be. Could it?

Woof! Nicole yelped and jumped away from the booth as a whimpering Magnus threw his body against her legs. Before she could catch him, Destin was standing right in front of her.

Shock registered on his face. "Nicole?" He looked over his shoulder, then trained his narrowed eyes on her. "What are you doing?"

Nicole held up her plastic bag. "Shopping," she said a little too quickly. His frown deepened at her innocent shrug.

"What ahhh…what are *you* doing?" she breathed, trying to keep her wildly beating heart in her chest. Her attention turned toward the curious couple now standing behind Destin, staring at her.

"Did you follow me?"

"What? No!" She shifted her weight. "I was looking for—" the booth was filled with fishing gear "—souvenirs."

Destin's smirk said he didn't believe her. He opened his mouth, probably to yell at her, when she looked over Destin's shoulder and saw her new acquaintance's eyes widen.

"Inspector Lima. Nice to see you again!" Nicole shouted over Destin's shoulder. She caught the brief, silent exchange between him and Destin.

Regrouping, the inspector nodded slightly. "Miss Parks. Hello. Please, call me Rui." Nicole saw the young woman's head swivel between them.

Destin jumped in, his body tense. "I didn't know you two knew each other."

"You didn't?" Nicole asked sharply.

"Of course, I told you Destin," Rui said smoothly, his smile plastic.

"You should have mentioned that you knew Destin when we saw each other yesterday," Nicole said to Rui. "I wouldn't have been so…forceful." She and Rui both chuckled uncomfortably. Destin's jaw clenched.

"I am Luiza," the young woman interrupted with a genuine smile for Nicole.

"Desculpa, meu amor." Rui sighed. "Miss Parks, this is my wife."

"Nice to meet you," Nicole said, feeling her jealousy abate at the word *wife*.

"You're American? From where?" Luiza asked.

"I'm from New York."

"Ahhh… Nova York. How do you know Destin?" Luiza smiled, glancing at Destin with a teasing look in her eye.

"She's working for my father." His serious tone cut through the conversation like a guillotine.

Nicole looked at Destin from the side of her eye. "Speaking of work. Have you two spoken about the winery?"

"Mmm-hmm," Destin and Rui said at the same time.

Mmm-hmm... "Because I stand by my findings. There are no earthquakes."

"What earthquakes?" Luiza interrupted, frowning at both Rui and Destin. The inspector's gaze hit the ground. Luiza gasped. "There was an earthquake at the factory? Why didn't I hear of this?"

Factory? "Um, your husband and his team predicted earthquakes would soon be hitting the winery."

Luiza's brows crunched. "There have never been earthquakes there," she said matter-of-factly. She slid a narrowed glance to her husband. "When were you at the winery?"

"He was helping me, Luiza," Destin interrupted softly. His gaze slide to Nicole's and those blue eyes were defiant.

Rui spoke Portuguese under his breath to Luiza, then put his arm around her. "Don't we have more to get at the market?" he asked loudly. The couple graciously excused themselves to continue their Sunday, leaving Destin and Nicole to stare at each other, the air dense with tension.

Nicole didn't know what was going on, but she knew one thing. Rui wasn't an inspector. With that realization, pieces fell into place—Destin badgering her for her schedule, lectures about the type of clientele best for Rio Grande...

Destin had tried to sabotage her meeting.

"Well, I guess Magnus and I should be going." Destin slapped his leg for the dog to follow and began a brisk walk away from the fair. Oh, no, he wasn't getting away that easy. She fell into step behind him.

"So Rui is a good friend?" Nicole started.

"Rui and Luiza used to work at the vineyard. Now they've moved on to other things," he tossed over his shoulder.

"You told Luiza Rui had been helping you. What's he been helping you do?"

"Odd jobs," he said quickly. They turned down an alleyway. "Should you be on that ankle?"

"I'm wearing a brace." Nicole spotted the Jeep. "Why are you running away from me?"

"I have work to do," he said, his hand on the car door.

"Plotting more sabotage?" she asked with deliberate innocence.

He whipped around and pinned her with a dangerous look. Slowly, he closed the distance between them. His chest rose and fell steadily, blocking out the rest of the world. She stood her ground. His blue gaze didn't waver as it traveled over her tank top and down to her shorts. Was he trying to intimidate her?

His smile was slow, and her heart beat a little faster as she watched the curve of his lips turn from amused to wicked, but that wasn't what had her blood pumping. Their bodies were talking. Their gazes were trained on each other's mouths. She could smell him—citrus, pine and outdoors.

Unable to focus, she took a step back, aware that the brick wall of the alley was just inches away.

"I like the braids," he murmured, touching one lightly.

She swallowed. It was an inconvenient pleasure to want him, especially when they had so much more to discuss.

She stepped forward, her breasts grazing his torso. His head lowered. Their lips were inches from each other. "You and your friend tried to sabotage my appointment. Wasn't that what the money was for?"

He stepped back with an exasperated sigh.

"I knew you didn't want to sell, but you crossed a line—"

"You crossed a line when you brought those people to my land," he said sharply.

"At your company's request!"

"At my father's request," he clarified in a snide tone.

"Well, I'll be sure to let him know how you feel."

"He knows how I feel. And you aren't telling him anything."

"You can't stop me!"

"Oh yes," he said in a low voice. "I can." His dark gaze said he meant it.

"Explain yourself," she spat.

His gaze searched the stone wall and came back to hers. "Dechamps France is in debt, and my father is exercising his right as majority shareholder to sell the land and keep the company solvent, regardless of my or Elliot's approval. He needs money now. So rebuilding Dechamps Brazil is not an option."

"Then why block the sale?"

"I'm keeping the land."

She blinked. "That's not possible. The listing is already out, and I have powerful people coming to buy. It's not a matter of if the land will sell, it's a matter of when. I'm not sure you can stop it at this point."

"I can stop it if I can raise the money to buy it myself."

Nicole blinked, unsure if she'd heard him correctly.

"Look, the inspection wasn't personal. I feel awful about it, but I can't lose that land. If I lose the land, I lose everything."

Nicole's eyes darted around the graffiti-covered walls, then came back to his intense stare. "Am I being punked?"

"No."

"No?" she repeated, her voice dripping with sarcasm. "So, what's your plan? Just sabotage every buyer who's interested in the land until you can raise the money?"

"It's worked so far."

Nicole's jaw dropped. Her promotion had just sprouted wings and flown away. And taken her adopted child with it.

"How long have you been doing this?" Her voice was weak, like she'd already lost the fight.

"Almost a year."

She needed to sit down. "Why, Destin? Why do this if you have no plans to rebuild?"

Silence. He crossed his arms over his chest. The vines she'd noticed popped into her head. As did the high-tech cask room.

"You're rebuilding and no one knows. Not even Elliot," she half whispered, wondering how she'd gotten herself into this mess.

"Elliot knows, but he will not get involved. He doesn't have as much at stake as I do. It's between our father and me."

"Destin, have you even talked to your father about this?"

"Of course."

"And?"

"And if I want to keep the land, I need to buy my father out and cover enough of the debt to raise the credit rating for a loan. Elliot has already promised me his shares if I can raise the money."

Nicole was silent for a moment, then her gaze flicked to his. "And with each failed sale, you're driving the price of the land down. Your father asked for fifty million last year. Now he'll settle for forty."

Destin gave her an impressed look. "I'm hoping that after we get through your clients, he'll entertain thirty million."

She shook her head at the audacity. Then grappled with the fact that he could actually do it, had *been* doing it. And it would be at her expense.

"I can't believe this. Do you have any idea what this could do to my career?"

"You won't get hurt. As long as you keep this to yourself, everything will work out." He said it with such confidence, she almost believed him.

"Destin, I know you've been through a lot. Maybe you haven't talked to the right people. I can help you and your father. I can talk to Clay. I can find you another parent company—"

"I won't get in bed with another company so they can burn me the way my father has. I have a plan, Nicole. You'll talk to no one."

She threw her hands in the air and shouted, "Well, if I'm not going to sell this land, I might as well leave!"

Destin's hand caught her arm, stopping her in her tracks. "Lower your voice."

"Why?" she snapped, trying to shake him off, aware he was too strong, even though his grip was gentle. "Everyone else is getting what they want." Her voice rose as she tried to yank her arm away. "What about what I want? Doesn't anyone care about me?"

With a small tug, he pulled her close and crashed his mouth against hers. It happened fast, but she was aware she was up against the alley wall, his hand at her nape, holding her in place as he licked the inside of her mouth. She made a small noise in her throat and traced her fingertips up his chest, tangling them in his hair. Gently, without breaking their kiss, he lowered himself, palmed her naked thighs and lifted her against the wall. Instinctually, she wrapped her legs around him.

Tenacious need rose and burned her from the inside out. There were no tentative touches this time, no silent calls for permission. He took and she gave, as much as they could while clothed, unable to withstand their pent-up needs any longer. She grabbed his head and kissed him, pushing her tongue into his mouth, rocking her lower body against him. He surged against her in a slow, dry hump that had her head flying back and his face buried in her cleavage. She arched her back for him, and he palmed her breasts over her top.

"You are torturing me," he whispered, thumbing her nipples over the fabric until they hardened against her bra. She heard his protest, as if he were acting against his will. In answer, she leaned down and kissed him deeper, longer, her tongue moving seductively over his.

He sank into the kiss, pushing his lower body against her more forcefully, tugging on her tank top until one perfect nipple was exposed. "I bet you taste like wine." Her thoughts were erased when he broke their kiss and closed his wet lips over the hardened tip.

On a gasp, she shoved her hands into his hair and tightened her legs around him, anchoring him to her breast. He sucked hard. In response, she rolled her hips against him, gritting her teeth against the pleasure and reveling in her power when his whole body shook.

Gently releasing her from his mouth, his slid his hands down her torso and over her butt, looking into her eyes as he pulled her against his straining erection.

He leaned in for another kiss. "You see my dilemma," he whispered against her mouth. "I can't be attracted to the woman working against me."

Another protest, she thought, although his body didn't seem to be having a problem knowing what it wanted.

"I can help you. You just won't let me." Her eyes were closed, and for a moment they were the only two people in the world.

"You can help me when I secure the land for myself." His lips found her neck and trailed a path from her ear to the hollow of her throat.

Her eyes opened slowly then, the realization that they'd been bickering, moments ago beginning to cut through the passionate haze. His lips claimed her again, his kiss deep and long, threatening to take her thoughts. She pulled her mouth from his.

"What happens if I don't go along with this plan?"

He blinked swiftly, as if doused with ice water. "I call your supervisor and say this isn't working out."

"Put me down," she commanded, pushing at his shoulders. He didn't budge, holding her in the steel of his arms.

"It doesn't have to come to that," he said gently, as if placating a child. "Do your job. I have this covered. It will work out in the end. For both of us."

"Put. Me. Down." She straightened her top and began to wiggle from his grasp.

With a heavy sigh, he pulled back his hips and lowered her carefully, untangling himself from her limbs, his dark gaze intense and still touched with arousal.

He took a few steps back and stood at a distance, struggling to regain control. She stared at him, confused, her lips parted, trying to catch her breath. "How do you know this will work?"

"I have investors lined up already. I just need more time." There was no inflection in his voice. He was going to execute this plan with or without her.

"I think I need to wrap my head around this."

She'd started walking down the other side of the alley when she felt a hand on her arm. "Let me take you back to the hotel."

Ignoring the heat of his palm, she broke his grasp and kept walking. "No. I know the way."

"I'll need your appointment schedule," he called after her.

She didn't look back.

Chapter 14

Monday morning Nicole woke restless and frustrated over Destin's threat to her job and her ardent attraction to him. She wasn't sure what was in store for her buyers, but giving Destin access to her appointments felt like handing him a grenade. And if she didn't go through with whatever his plan was, Destin would call her boss and get her replaced. Could he do that without his father's knowledge? She didn't want to find out.

The morning sun burst happily through the lace curtains, and the weather app on her phone indicated no signs of rain or storms. Three showings sat on her calendar for the day, but she burrowed farther under her covers, avoiding the question that loomed like a black cloud. Did she tell Destin about them? Or did she show the land behind Destin's back?

The look in his eyes when he'd told her he had plans to rebuild had been so earnest, almost pleading. And how humiliating her response to his kiss in the alley had been.

It was as if every time she saw him, her body hijacked her mind and overwhelmed her senses. She hated him and wanted him, and hated herself for giving in so easily. But kissing him had been delicious…and disastrous.

She fluffed a pillow and rolled onto her side, trying to get away from the confusion in her mind.

The phone in her room rang. She glanced at the clock and grimaced. The only person who ever dared call her this early was Gustavo. She picked up the receiver with a murmured hello.

"Good morning," said a deep voice.

Not Gustavo. She rolled onto her back. "A little early, isn't it?"

"I've been up for hours. I told you, the life of a vintner isn't glamorous. Did I wake you?"

"No, I'm awake." And picturing him at his château in a towel. Maybe it was the phone, but his voice and accent were more pronounced. Penetrating. There was that feeling again, like all she wanted to do was offer herself for his pleasure. She cleared her throat. "What can I do for you?"

"I need your schedule."

His hotness was forgotten just like that. "Schedule?"

"Your clients, Nicole. Or have you forgotten our discussion?"

"I think that's called blackmail."

A heavy sigh came through the phone. "Think of it as a partnership that will work in your favor."

"Partners," she repeated.

"You see? It's better."

"Right." She hesitated. Made a split-second decision. "Okay, partner. They're all tomorrow in three-hour increments, starting at noon."

"More casinos?"

"A spa company, a mannequin and toy manufacturer,

and a data storage company. Are those more palatable for you?"

"It won't matter."

"Then I guess you won't want to hear about the others that want to come in next week." Since her cell service had been restored, she'd gotten messages from more interested buyers. Something she would have been ecstatic over, had she not been aware of Destin's plan.

"Christ," he cursed. "Later. Right now we'll focus on tomorrow."

"Are you going to send clowns this time? Maybe a pack of wolves to chase us off the place?"

He chuckled. "Don't wear your heels. Just in case. Enjoy your day."

Oh, I will, she thought after he abruptly hung up. Jumping from the bed, she showered, ordered breakfast to her room and sifted through her files. Today was a big day, and Destin wasn't going to be a distraction.

Thirty minutes before her first appointment, Nicole set up shop at the bar in the hotel restaurant. She was filling in Gustavo when Anton walked behind the bar and poured her more water. Her light blazer lay on the stool beside her.

"Yes, all three are today. The storm had everyone rescheduling on top of each other." *Thank you*, she mouthed to Anton.

"Have you heard from Clay?"

"He sent an offer, but you know Clay, he loves to negotiate. Came in way too low, which I rejected. I didn't even send it to Elliot. I'm waiting on round two."

"Have you seen his Instagram feed?"

"No. This is the first time I've had consistent cell service since the storm."

"He's been posing around the city with a machete."

She shook her head. "He's still in town, so that's a good sign."

"You're right. I have every bit of faith you'll bring this home, Nicole." She closed her eyes and squeezed the bridge of her nose. *I'm glad one of us does.* "Thanks, boss."

She hung up and had started sifting through her emails when another offer from Clay popped through. It was a second bid, not quite at asking price, but close, with a contingency for more upon seeing the inside of the wine cellar. Nicole forwarded the email to Elliot with a note for him to call her and smiled to herself. It was all coming together.

"Lunch for you?" Anton asked.

"No, thank you, I had a huge breakfast. I can't eat when I'm working." Nicole turned back to her laptop but stopped when she realized Anton was still standing there.

"Big day today?" he asked.

"I'm showing some buyers the Dechamps property," she said, glancing outside to make sure that the van she'd hired was still idle and waiting.

The second Destin's last name left her lips, the feel of his muscles and the grip of his hands came back to her. She quickly grabbed her water and washed those thoughts down her throat. She didn't want to think about him. Not now, while she was going behind his back.

A car pulled up and out stepped three young people in colorful robes with crystals hanging from their necks. Then she saw the smaller, fragile stature of Seguay; his stringy gray hair was pulled back into a ponytail and the others waited for him to walk by, then fell into a triangle formation behind him. His hands were steepled, and the group bowed to Nicole after crossing the threshold into the restaurant.

Twenty-five years ago, Ira Goldberg from the Bronx went to India looking for enlightenment and returned to America a year later renamed "Seguay to the light,"

Seguay for short. He relocated to Costa Rica and started a yoga retreat, which blew up into an empire based on healing, wellness and spiritual education.

He'd been on Oprah, done a TED talk about collective consciousness and written a bestselling book on the same subject. Celebrities had publicly thanked him for saving their souls. He'd opened branches in Mexico and California, and was looking for the next place to spread his message. Should be a sure thing, except Seguay wouldn't consult a real estate developer, just his gurus. If the wind blew the wrong way or one of his gurus caught bad vibes, the deal was off.

Seguay rose first. "Miss Parks, so nice to see you. *Namaste.*" Quickly, Nicole slid off her stool and executed a small bow back, feeling a little like she was in the presence of Jesus. The group rose and bowed again. Nicole turned to find Anton standing behind the bar staring. She almost laughed at the look on his face.

"*Namaste*, Seguay. Wonderful to see you. I hope your trip has been pleasant so far."

Seguay came forward and hugged Nicole—for a little too long. When he stepped back, his hands were up and his eyes were closed. "Your aura is clear, except…" His gaze went to her ankle. "You've hurt yourself. But it's healing, and you'll be fine."

How did he know that? Nicole's eyes widened briefly, then she fixed a smile on her face and nodded. "Thank you. Is there anything you and your…" she looked to the people in robes "…team want to discuss before we head up to the land? I have a van waiting for us."

"We've been walking around reading the energy of the city all morning. Such robust spirit. We are in the perfect mindset to see the land. We can talk business after." Seguay took Nicole's hand as they walked to the van. "Tell me, how is your love life?"

Nicole spent the next forty minutes dodging that question. They had to take the long route up the mountain, past Destin's château, because the other route still wasn't clear of the large tree that had fallen during the storm.

They pulled up to the front gate, and without a word, Seguay popped out of the van first.

"Seguay, you have to go through the—" Nicole cut herself off as Seguay shot through the trees. His team scrambled behind him.

When Nicole emerged from the trail, Seguay was meditating on the ground while his three companions were holding their crystals and walking the property with their eyes closed. She tiptoed, scanning the area for Destin, waiting for something crazy to happen.

Not that it got crazier than this.

One of the gurus stopped and turned to the forest where Destin's vines were hidden. "There is life here!" she shouted and began to step toward it.

Nicole rushed forward. "I wouldn't go in there. There is life in there, for sure. Animals that don't want us messing with their habitat. At least, not until someone moves in."

Seguay stood. "I can feel the tragedy here. We will have to clear this place."

Nicole thought that meant they were leaving. Instead, Seguay and his team converged on the rubble of the main house, surrounded it, and began to hum. One lit a sage bundle and walked in a circle.

She wondered if Destin was hiding and watching, laughing.

The "clearing" went on for some time. Nicole checked her watch, then tiptoed behind Seguay. "I'm so sorry, but we'll need to leave soon," she whispered.

Seguay turned slowly. "I want to speak to the one that makes the wines."

"Mmm, okay," she said in a smooth voice that disguised

her apprehension. Did he know about the wines the way he knew about her ankle? "There are no more wines, if that's what you're looking for."

Seguay's eyes narrowed. "There needs to be, or this place won't heal. I've had a vision of a retreat with sustainable food and wine. Macrobiotic. Biodynamic. Everything of the earth." He stopped and turned. "Reach out to the vintner for me. Give him my direct line. Not Elliot. The other one. Destin, I think."

Nicole's eyes widened and she held her breath. He *was* Jesus.

Seguay chuckled at her reaction. "I speak to the universe. But I have Google, too."

The ride down the mountain was quiet, as Seguay needed to meditate, which meant the rest of the team meditated, as well. They dropped Nicole off at the hotel, and Seguay promised to send an offer. "But I want to speak to the vintner first."

Nicole felt the loss of the sale, knowing that even if she told Destin about Seguay's "vision," he'd never call. She bid them all goodbye and was about to shut the door when Seguay spoke again, his gray gaze sharp.

"You'll heal him, you know. It's already happening."

She didn't ask who he referred to. Simply nodded and shut the door to the van.

What the hell had just happened? Normally she'd have time to process, but her next appointment was already waiting for her in the lobby of the hotel. Mr. William Randall and his agent, Marcus, both from California, were friendly but all business. Neither seemed interested in Rio Grande or the people in it.

"We need space to build a factory," William stated as they rode up the mountain.

"Yes, of course. What do you manufacture, again?" Nicole feigned forgetfulness out of courtesy. Mr. Randall had never actually told her what he manufactured, and there wasn't much information about him online. His company was obscure, but the bank documents showed he'd made a fortune selling mannequins, with most of his revenue coming from the German, Australian and UK markets.

"Lots of things."

"Toys."

The men spoke at the same time.

Nicole's gaze darted between the two, who both looked a bit waxen under her scrutiny. Her smile waned a bit. "Oh, toys. What kind?"

"Things for adults," Marcus said quickly, before turning his focus out the window. Why were they acting so strange?

"Like board games?" she asked, refusing to give up."

"Well, yes, we have some board games but mostly dolls."

Nicole cocked her head.

"Sex dolls," Mr. Randall snapped. Marcus's lips tightened.

The van stopped short, and the driver began yelling at someone outside his window.

"Excuse me." *Sex dolls!* She could hear Destin's lecture now.

Nicole unbuckled herself from her seat and poked her head into the front. Cows. They were everywhere. Their black-and-white bodies bellowed as they surrounded the van and blocked the road.

The driver laid on the horn, but the cows didn't budge.

"Oh, my God. What do we do?"

The driver shrugged, then pointed to several more cows sauntering down the road to join the herd. And there wasn't a farmer in sight. According to the driver, they had another twenty minutes to go up the mountain. Walking was not an option. If they couldn't get those cows to move, they'd have to turn around.

She couldn't believe what was happening. With the calm demeanor of a flight attendant, Nicole turned to her clients and relayed the problem.

"I grew up in Montana," Marcus said, taking off his suit jacket. "Let me handle this." He rolled up his sleeves, slid open the door, then jumped to the ground, slapping the cows to get them moving. After a minute of no progress, he began walking through the herd, clapping his hands and making weird barking noises.

Nicole climbed into the front and watched from the passenger seat as a few cows moved, only to be replaced by more.

"Should he be sliding behind them like that?" Nicole asked with a grimace.

"No," said the driver. And, sure enough, as the three of them watched, Marcus got a full kick to the chest from one of the cows. They all shouted as his body shook, then crumpled to the ground. The driver was the first to jump out, and with William's help, they laid Marcus down in the back of the van. He was conscious and, judging by the way he was holding his chest and rolling back and forth, in acute pain.

They sideswiped a cow as they backed up the vehicle and raced to the hospital. X-rays showed two broken ribs and a nasty black bruise spreading over Marcus's torso. She felt horrible, and when Marcus was finally bandaged and sleeping, she apologized to Mr. Randall for the mishap and said she hoped he would reschedule a viewing soon.

The look he gave her said she would never hear from him again.

Understood.

On the drive back to the hotel, Nicole realized that with both of the roads now blocked, she had no time to wait for them to clear and no choice but to cancel her third appointment. Destin would be ecstatic.

Hold the phone, Nicole thought as her driver pulled up to the hotel. Could Destin have had something to do with cowmania back there? He did say he had a friend with a farm. *Impossible*, she thought as she headed for the restaurant. Unless he had seen her earlier at the property, he couldn't know. Surely it was just bad luck. Kind of like this whole trip so far.

She checked the time. She had an hour until her next appointment. Without access to those roads, she was screwed. And she couldn't reschedule them for Tuesday; that was Destin's sabotage day. She should just fly home now...

"That's it!" A brilliant idea came to her, but she didn't know how to execute it. She looked around for help but came up empty. She went out to the lobby. "Anton?"

Anton was just getting off the phone and looked a little frazzled.

"How can I help you, Miss Parks?"

She placed both hands on the counter and leaned forward, aware her request was a little insane. "I need a helicopter. Now."

Her luck was turning. Nicole and her last buyers of the day soared over the forest treetops and reveled in the bird's-eye view of the inlet waterfalls, the bottomless canyons and the ocean's never-ending reach across the earth. Jagged-edged rocks crawled far down the face of the oceanside cliff and faded into perfect white sand.

"This is fucking epic!" Jared Seagram, the twenty-five-year-old CEO of a two-hundred-million-dollar data storage start-up called WhoDat, flipped the bill of his baseball cap up so he could get closer to the window. He and his even younger CFO, who was wearing a T-shirt that said "Baller," high-fived and snapped a selfie.

Millennials. "We should be coming up on Dechamps!" Nicole shouted, hoping they understood her over their headgear.

Leaning forward, she looked out the window and watched as they flew over a long white tarp. More forest appeared underneath them, then a larger patch of several long white tarps. They blew past the tarps and hit more trees. Nicole looked around for land markers but didn't recognize anything.

She pulled out her GPS and saw the tag for Dechamps behind them.

"We passed it. Turn around!" she shouted to the pilot. With a nod, he pulled an air U-turn, and they flew back toward the marker. Her phone beeped when they hit the white tarp again.

Confused, she looked again, her mind unable to process what was flying by right under her.

All of Dechamps had been covered with a tent.

She looked at her clients and gave a tentative smile, still trying to process how the land could have been concealed in less than a few hours. And why?

She wanted to curse out loud. She wanted to jump out of that chopper and tear that tarp apart.

She wanted to find Destin. He must have found out. But how?

Mind racing with what to say, she turned to her young buyers. "It looks like the place has been covered. We, uh... can't see anything."

Both lost their smiles.

Nicole asked the pilot to turn around and return them to the helipad. After an embarrassing explanation, Nicole avoided eye contact with the "ballers," looking out over the cliff instead. They passed a group of homes, and Nicole gasped when she recognized Destin's château. As they got closer, she could see the back patio.

And there he was, sitting barefoot in the shade, in a blue T-shirt and sunglasses. A bottle of wine was chilling in a silver bucket next to him. He smiled and raised his glass to the helicopter.

She wanted him. She hated him…

But mostly she hated him.

Chapter 15

Hotel Mystique was the hottest, most elegant and most extravagant hotel in the city, and it had been built for the sole purpose of attracting the elite. No wonder Clay wanted to have drinks there. She'd gotten his call shortly after her last appointment, inviting both her and Elliot out for a friendly cocktail. She wasn't in the mood, but you never said no to a buyer who had made an offer, and since Elliot couldn't make it, she had no choice.

Designed by an apprentice of Frank Lloyd Wright's, the exterior of the hotel was in the shape of a cruise ship and fashioned with circular windows, underwater propellers that slowly spun and hanging life rafts that could be reserved for play.

Every night the glitterati handed their Range Rovers and Mercedes Benzes off to young valets and followed the red carpet inside to the rooftop, which looked like a real ship's deck. Tall masts, a giant ship's wheel and large silver sails flew in the breeze, all under a starry night sky.

Nicole slid through the beautiful crowd, watching the partiers dance in their spots as a pop song played in the background. To her left, the bar itself acted as a beacon in the dark, glowing white, then purple, then red. The drinks on the bar looked ethereal.

If she hadn't known better, she could've tricked herself into thinking she was back in New York. No spiders, no mud roads, no Destin—and he had been the reason for what had probably been the worst day in her career.

She'd been humiliated at her last two appointments. Her phone calls and emails of apology to both had gone unanswered. And, of course, there was Gus, who sounded concerned that things were getting out of hand. Making the sale was one thing, keeping the company's reputation as the best was another. People in hospitals were not a good advertisement.

After she'd hung up with her boss, she'd set out to give Destin a curse-filled piece of her mind, only to quickly realize she didn't have his phone number, or email, or a horse that could jump cows and bust through his château door. He'd won, just like he'd said he would.

To lift her spirits, she'd put extra glam into her appearance that night. She was going to enjoy herself, Destin Dechamps be damned. Her off-the-shoulder stretch lace dress hugged her body and was opaque only across the chest and the skirt. She wore gold eyeshadow, red lipstick, her hair in a bun and shimmer lotion on her legs. Ignoring her better judgment, she'd gone with heels and planned to sit most of the time.

Cocktail waitresses carried bottles on silver trays, and Nicole followed one until she spotted Clay's white Stetson. He stood in his cowboy boots talking to a beautiful Brazilian woman. Next to him, Chuck and Diane sipped drinks on a velvet couch.

"Nicole! Get over here." Clay turned with a drink in his hand and squished her in his signature bear hug.

"Having fun, Clay?"

"This is genius. It looks like my daddy's yacht! I was just thinking. We could build the casino to look like a pirate ship! Then we can keep the haunted house. And the wine cellar could be like a pirate's den!"

Nicole slid a glance at Chuck, who raised his eyebrows and tipped his Stetson her way. Yeah, he'd heard this already.

"Clay, if they take your bid, you can do whatever you want. You could buy real pirates if you wanted to."

Clay stilled. "Wait, you think I could find some real pirates around here? Chuck!" Chuck didn't budge. "Chuck! Goddamn it," Clay muttered after another try. "It's too loud in here."

"Yep." Nicole smirked as Chuck continued to turn away.

"So, what did they think of the offer?" Clay asked with barely leashed excitement.

"They were pleased, but you know how this goes. Someone may want it more than you."

"Nicole." Clay got serious. "No one wants it more than me. Remember that."

"May I ask why you want it so bad?"

"People need to have fun."

Nicole looked around. "This looks pretty fun."

"I mean rich people. Billionaires."

"So your pirate ship casino could be a playground for wealthy tourists." A vision of a sunburned Clay lounging on the deck of his "pirate ship" surrounded by Brazilian beauties in bikinis popped into her mind.

"Bingo. An exotic destination, like Atlantis in the Bahamas."

Nicole thought of Destin's lecture on what was good for Rio Grande.

"Well, you certainly have vision, Clay."

His chest puffed. "That's what my daddy says. Enough shop talk. Let's get you a drink. Hey, little lady!" Clay shouted at a pretty server.

Clay ordered a round of caipirinhas for the table, Brazil's national cocktail. They were made with cachaça, sugar and lime poured over ice. After clinking their glasses together, they all took their first sip. Diane's lips pursed. Chuck held his breath as he swallowed. And Clay yelled, "Wooo! This drink is strong!"

Nicole let the liquid slide down her throat, then blew out a calming breath. She'd had her share of exotic liquors. In New Orleans it had been absinthe. Mexico, tequila. Chile, pisco. Cachaça? It tasted like a blend of all of the above, on steroids.

Clay pursed his lips and slapped his thigh after another sip. "Chuck! We are taking a case of cachaça home!"

The conversation stayed light, with talk of Clay's family, his dog and the new home he'd bought in Texas. Diane stared daggers every time Clay's eyes strayed over a pair of legs that walked by. And the drunker Diane got, the less she hid her disdain, especially since Clay refused to look at her.

Nicole smelled an affair and a fight coming on. Plus, her polite smile was getting tired. As much as she liked Clay and was having a good time, all she could think about was Destin.

She caught herself looking at every dark-haired male on the roof, either wishing it was Destin or forming a comparison. She told herself she wanted to talk more about his interference, but her mind always wandered to his mouth on hers and his body between her legs against the stone wall of the alley.

She wanted him. Even after the shenanigans of the day, she yearned to see him again. It was torture.

Excusing herself to the bathroom, she walked toward the back of the deck and, instead of dipping into the ladies' lounge, found an empty spot at the balcony.

A blanket of stars twinkled over the man-made lights of the city. She stretched on her tiptoes to locate the ocean, wondering what Destin was doing under the same stars. Laughing at her while sipping wine on his terrace, maybe? Congratulating himself on a well-executed plan of ruin?

How had she gotten herself into this mess? Destin was an obstacle she didn't know how to handle, especially since her feelings were so muddled. His family was her client, so any accusations she made against him could jeopardize a multimillion-dollar deal for Dechamps, her company and her reputation.

Playing along seemed like the best option, as long as she could still make a deal under the radar. Destin had won this last battle, but she still had the casino. Clay was unpredictable, and that might prove to be an advantage.

After a visit to the lounge, Nicole made her way back to the couches, stepping around a large party. Scanning the dense crowd, she slowed, her heart racing as Destin's unmistakable profile appeared just a few feet away. Drink in hand, he stood with a group of men, his head thrown back in laughter.

Her blood pumped and she stood still, paralyzed by the simultaneous urge to be next to him and the instinct to sprint away. The crowd jostled in front of her, teasing her with glimpses of his tall frame. Like a stalker, she watched, waiting for something. A sign, maybe?

Then it happened. With a slight turn of his head, his gaze settled in her direction. He did a double take, the heat of his gaze traveling over her dress. Quickly, she looked away and kept going, bumping right into a man dancing wildly. "I'm so sorry. Excuse—" Before she knew it, Destin was there, pulling her out of the congestion to the other side of the roof deck.

He looked amazing. Dashing. His thick dark hair curled at the ends, and his beard was trimmed. He wore a black button-down rolled at the sleeves, jeans and black leather Converse high-tops. Playboy chic.

"Well, this is a surprise," she said, feeling a little off balance at how blue his eyes looked. She nearly swooned when he pulled her in close for a kiss on each cheek. He squared his shoulders, blocking out the crush of people behind them.

"What are you doing here?" His voice was gruff.

Her chin went up. "So nice to see you too, Destin. For the second time today," she added, her voice dripping with sarcasm.

His eyebrows rose, and the slightest smile touched his mouth. "Did you follow me here?" he asked, his fingers grazing her shoulder to brush at a tendril that had come loose from her bun.

"Get over yourself. I'm here with a buyer. And don't," she said, slapping his hand away. "I'm mad at you."

"I'm mad at you, too," he said bluntly. "But I have a feeling I'm going to get over it." His gaze dipped to her dress. "You look beautiful."

A shiver ran up her spine. Where the hell was her drink? "Compliments won't work. You tried to ruin me today."

"And you tried to lie to me today," he said, drinking deeply from his cocktail. "I think we're even."

"How did you know?" Elliot was the only other person who had her schedule, but their conversation earlier had given her the impression that he and Destin weren't communicating.

"Let's just say I have friends in high places. Did you

like the helicopter? I kind of wish I could have been there. Genius, by the way. I didn't see that one coming."

"But you were able to thwart it, anyway. Good for you."

He tipped his drink to his mouth and stared at her over his glass for a long moment. His gaze briefly dropped to her lips. "I won't apologize."

"I'd die of shock if you did."

Bass music surrounded them, emphasizing the palpable anger that was in the air. As if pulled, he moved closer, and she held back a powerful urge to touch him.

"We can't have that, now, can we? You shouldn't be on that ankle." He glanced at her shoes. "Be careful. I didn't bring my knife tonight."

"Thank you, doctor, but my ankle is fine." She showed him with a little twist of her black pump, ignoring the small twinge of pain at the joint.

"Who are you here with?" he asked, his voice low and impatient. "The casino?"

She gave him a sharp look. "Yes, the one buyer I have left, no thanks to you." Her mind ran through scenarios where she told Destin about the pirate ship idea and he threw Clay overboard.

"And have they made an offer?"

"Not yet," she lied, not giving up without a fight.

"So, what are you doing here with them?"

"Just drinks. I haven't seen Clay in a while—"

"Clay? That's a name?"

"Don't be petty."

Destin looked over her head. "Where are they?"

No, she was not going to introduce them. "Destin, they want to see inside the cellar. I need the keys."

Indignation registered on his face for a moment, then a smile spread across his face, one that could only be described as devious. And sexy as hell. He leaned in closer and let his gaze flicker to her mouth. "What would you do for them?"

The music turned into a heavier beat, and patrons around them danced and shook. Unable to resist his allure, she moved her lips inches from his. "I'd eat rabbit."

He smiled. She smiled. Aching for his kiss, her world turned in slow motion as he came forward.

"*Vin amante*! Destin! Come on, man, have another!" The man behind Destin stopped short when he saw Nicole. "Oh, wow. *Ciao, bella.*" Destin quickly straightened. Handsome and lean, with honey-colored hair and an impeccably tailored suit, Nicole could have guessed he was Italian before he had even said *ciao*.

Destin's friend came forward with a big smile and bounced excitedly in his Adidas Stan Smiths. "Introduce us, Desty. Introduce us."

Destin closed his eyes then popped them open. "Antonio, this is Nicole. Nicole, this is my friend Antonio. We've known each other since university."

"Nice to meet you, Nicole. Call me Toni," he said, holding out his hand.

"You too, Toni. A pleasure."

Toni leaned toward Destin excitedly. "Oooh. She's American. Now we're like, the United Nations. Nicole, how does a gorgeous woman like yourself know this lump?"

Nicole looked to Destin, who was staring over her head. She hoped he wasn't looking for Clay.

"We don't know each other that well," she said, intent on getting in one last dig. Destin's gaze snapped to her.

"*Eccellente*, that means you and I can get to know each other." Toni smiled.

Destin turned to his friend with a murderous look and said something under his breath that made Toni's eyebrows go up and a sly smile cross his face.

"You old dog. It's about time. My sister will be heartbroken," Toni said with a wink. Destin's frown deepened. "Come, Nicole, we've forgotten our manners. You need a drink." Toni held out his arm.

Nicole looked between the two men, who began speaking in Portuguese, noting Destin's pained look. She didn't know what they were saying, but whatever it was, it was about her. It was also obvious that Destin didn't want her to meet his friends.

"No, I should get back to my party."

"Nonsense," Toni said, taking her hand and leading her past a brooding Destin. "One drinky-poo." Suddenly she was led into a small group of very attractive and, judging by the bottle of Macallan 18 sitting out, clearly very wealthy young men. "*Attenzione*. This is Destin's friend, Nicole. She's off limits, so behave yourselves." Toni laughed and held his glass up. Destin shook his head. A drink came at her from another smiling hottie, who introduced the rest of their crew. She felt like she was in a living, breathing Gap ad.

Through the introductions, she learned that most of the calendar boys worked in private equity. Toni, however, was an international wine distributor with several warehouses in France and Italy, and one in São Paulo.

"Are you coming to the party later?" A slim African man asked Nicole after their introductions.

"What party?"

"No, I'm sure she can't. Nicole is here on business for my family," said a familiar deep voice behind her.

"Oh," her new friend said, then he jerked his head back with an enlightened "Oh!" before slinking away.

Unbelievable. Apparently, Destin had told all of his friends she was a leper. She'd been going to say no anyway, but the fact that Destin was towering above her like a brooding statue, and speaking for her, was just rude.

She whipped around and was surprised at how close he was standing. "So I'm uninvited to the party?"

"It's not a party, just a guys' night out. You wouldn't like it."

"You wouldn't know what I like," she said in soft reproach.

"I have a very good idea of what you like."

There it was again, that magnetic pull of their lips wanting to meet, but neither of them moved. Nicole dropped her gaze, trying to get a hold on her rampant lust. Maybe in other circumstances they would have had a chance, but right here and right now, they were at opposite ends of the spectrum. There was no trust.

"Good night, Destin."

With a wave to the Gap crew, she carefully made her way through the crowd.

"Nicole! *Rallenta*. Wait!" Recognizing the Italian accent, Nicole turned to see Toni coming at her with a lopsided grin. *Wild* and *charming* were the two words that came to mind, and possibly *single* since he wore no rings. Not that she was interested. Discreetly checking out a man's ring finger was a bad habit she'd like to break, but she would bet money on his having a few girlfriends. Maybe even all at the same time.

"Do not go to this address later tonight," he said, looking over his shoulder before handing her a small card. *Vin Amante*, it read. There was a wine glass drawn underneath. An address with GPS coordinates was on the back. "We will not be having fun there. Don't go," he said, backing away with a wicked grin. "I warned you."

"Hey, what is *Vin Amante*?" she shouted, but he was already gone. It sounded like a strip club.

Shaking her head, she put the card in her purse. Reverse psychology be damned. She wasn't going to that party to watch Destin throw dollar bills at high-class strippers. If

Destin had wanted her there, he would have invited her. It was the least he could have done after ruining her appointments and possibly her career.

Taking a deep breath, she went in search of Clay, unsure how much longer she could put on a happy face. Stripping off her dress, running cold water over her achy ankle and crying a little seemed like the night's most appealing options. When she found Clay, he was standing and holding onto a very drunk Diane.

"There you are, girl, I thought you went overboard." Clay laughed at his own joke. "Diane is wrecked. I think we gotta call it a night."

"No worries, Clay. I'm just going to finish this drink and head out, too."

"Are you sure? I can stay with ya." He looked around at the crowd. "Maybe I should stay."

Nicole took a gulp of her drink. "Go. I'll be done in two seconds. I'll be okay, I promise." Nicole let her gaze drift to the back corner, and she caught a glimpse of Destin, watching her.

"On second thought, I'll take this downstairs. So I'll walk out with you."

It took about fifteen minutes just to get down to the lobby, as Diane kept kicking off her shoes in the hallway and the elevator. Nicole stopped when they got to the quiet lobby lounge.

"I'm gonna hear from ya soon about our offer?"

"You betcha."

Clay gave her a big hug and a kiss on the cheek, then hauled Diane over his shoulder like a sack of potatoes. Chuck tipped his hat with one of Diane's shoes.

What a night. Nicole slid into an empty leather chair and sipped her drink. She didn't even know what it was, but it was delicious. Boys' night out, huh? It sounded crazy, but it was nice to see Destin enjoying time with his friends. He deserved happiness, she supposed.

Finishing her drink, she rose and walked outside to find a valet. She was tipping the young man and getting into her car when she saw them.

The group, in button-down shirts and fancy shoes, walked outside like a scene from *Swingers*. Her eyes followed Destin, and she studied the way he talked animatedly with his hands. She guessed it was time for strippers and debauchery.

She, however, was ready to go home. Not to the hotel. To New York.

She quickly drove by, praying Destin didn't recognize the SUV, but was caught behind a line of cars inching toward the exit. She watched half of the men pile into Destin's Jeep, while the other half got into a sleek red car. They were two vehicles behind her. Finally, she reached the exit and turned right, glancing furtively in her rearview; she saw Destin's Jeep turn left.

Don't you dare. Don't do it.

What was that wine-glass logo doing on that card?

It's none of your business.

But she was already making a U-turn.

Chapter 16

This is wrong, intrusive. You remember what happened last time you followed him? Turn around, said a voice in her head.

You were invited, said another. Her foot never left the gas.

She slowed when Destin and his friends did, twisting and turning through the narrow streets. Nicole wasn't sure where they were going, but she could tell they were getting farther away from the city center.

Lighting was scarce, but there was enough to see the trash that lined the sidewalks and the graffiti on the storefronts. Rusted bicycles were chained against the walls and neon-colored apartments were stacked on top of each other like Legos. They'd crossed into a favela, she was almost sure of it. She should turn around.

Just a little farther, said that inner voice.

Destin's Jeep took a sharp left into a dirt parking lot filled with cars. Nicole rolled her SUV to a stop beside a shadowed wall. Before her, people in a long line were waiting to get into a closed-off warehouse with no roof. Clouds of smoke and multicolored lights rose into the air, and muffled club music could be heard.

Two doormen lifted a velvet rope as Destin and his boy band approached. They disappeared inside while others were checked and waved away. She'd go in, take a look around and go home. He didn't need to know she was there. She could keep her distance and stay lost in the crowd.

Nicole parked her SUV, dabbed on her lipstick and confidently walked up to the velvet rope. She'd charmed her way into her share of New York clubs; getting past these two doormen should be a piece of cake.

Neither spoke English. She told them her name, then dropped Destin's as well. When she got blank stares, she flashed the card Toni had given her. To her relief, one of the doormen lifted the velvet rope. Nicole stepped inside and a samba/hip-hop hybrid filled her ears and rattled her chest. Electric lighting flashed over sweaty bodies that were gyrating against one another. A lone DJ manipulated turntables and laptops on a platform above the crowd. Behind him, a wall-sized digital counter was displayed, the numbers gradually increasing in small amounts.

Women in black tank tops poured drinks behind a long bar, and the surrounding haze was a mixture of dry ice and smoke.

Now, this was a party.

Nicole scanned the crowd for Destin. The sheer size of the place made it difficult. How was she supposed to avoid him if she didn't know where he was? She dipped down and worked her way across the room toward a dark corner. Feeling too exposed, she pushed her way through the throng by the bar.

"He'll shit when he finds out you're here." Toni. She whirled around.

"So don't tell him."

"Lie to my best friend that enemy number one has infiltrated our party?"

"Then you shouldn't have invited me. And I am not his enemy!"

"I said don't come," he teased. "And aren't you the big bad wolf out to steal his land?"

"You mean sell. And it's not his."

"Only on paper." He pointed to the counter. "But it will be."

"He's crowdfunding?"

"Among other things."

The counter barely read six figures. "I hate to break it to you, but that's not enough."

"That's what me and the others are here for, *bella*. And that's just for today."

Impressive. As was his boyish face. "You realize you have to promise something in return."

"You obviously haven't read our little donation list." He took one from the bar and handed it to her. "Here, should I put you down for, I don't know, a thousand? Or is that a conflict of interest?"

She ignored the barb. "According to this, my donation gets me a small stake in the winery."

"And two free cases of wine a year. Don't forget that one. Bartender?" He held up two fingers.

"Is he serious?"

"Dead serious. Profit sharing is important to him."

"What else is important to him?" Two shots of a clear liquid appeared.

"You, apparently. A few strategic calls to your company could have had you back in New York days ago. He's quite concerned with how you'll fare in all of this."

"You seem irritated by that. Should I just pack up and leave Brazil, then?"

"Yes. I like to know that my investment isn't in jeopardy. But you can stay for one drink." He winked and gave her a shot. They clinked. *"Salute."*

She gritted her teeth as the cachaça went down her throat.

The Italian looked into the crowd, then back to her with a smirk. "And now you can have a dance."

She looked around. Back, forth, back, spin, side to side. It was serious choreography that several couples around them had mastered—so much so that they put a sexy spin on it. A dip here, a booty roll there. Nicole was struggling to keep up. She could do a mean two-step, and a twerk or two, but what she was seeing was ballroom-type stuff with a dirty twist.

The music turned slower, sexier, and she began pulling away.

"That was fun!" she shouted. "But—"

Toni spun her around again, and when she stopped, she was staring at a familiar couple. Not five feet away from them, Destin was dancing with Thereza, and she was all over him.

"Oh." Toni feigned surprise beside her. "Look who it is. What do you say, Bella, one more dance?"

He gave her a knowing look, and a mischievous smile spread across his face. He was doing this on purpose, but she was fighting off jealousy and didn't care. She nodded. Toni spun her again so his back was against hers, and he bent to her ear.

"Just follow my lead."

Thereza's body snaked down Destin's again. He pulled his pelvis away slightly when she turned and slinked back. She was extra-aggressive tonight. Because she was the sister of his best friend, he'd humor her—he caught her palm as she reached between his legs—to a point.

Usually he didn't dance, but tonight he was celebrating. His investors were lined up, the crowdfunding was a success, and his father had no buyer prospects. The land was going to be his. He could feel it.

Then there was Nicole. She'd looked so beautiful at Hotel Mystique that, when she'd walked away, it was all he could do to keep his eyes off her and that huge blond American. His interference with her appointments had her angry, and rightfully so, but seeing that uncertainty in her eyes almost killed him. She didn't deserve to be in the middle of this.

She didn't know it yet, but when Destin was ready to make an offer, he wanted her to present it to his father. She'd still get credit for the sale, and honestly, he trusted no one else to make sure any contracts between himself and his father were fair. It would work out for both of them, as he'd promised. Nicole could go home assured of a promotion.

Destin stopped midstep. Thereza frowned.

Shaking off the ominous feeling that washed over him, Destin spun Thereza to arm's length, then twirled her back in, remembering most of the samba steps his wife had taught him. Thereza, however, seemed to be auditioning for *Dancing with the Stars*. She tossed her hair and licked her lips, executing a move that had her breasts threatening to spill out from her tight dress.

It was time to find her brother.

He looked around frantically, holding Thereza away from him as she backed it up and rolled her hips toward his pelvis again. Where the hell was Toni?

Destin stilled. He saw Nicole's legs before his gaze fixated on the back of her lace dress. She was staring at her feet, but doing a good job of keeping up with Toni. His friend spun Nicole once, then again, which had her smiling. Her hips swung with each step, and her legs shimmered.

Never had Destin felt jealousy so intense, especially after the warning he'd given Toni at the hotel. Nicole was not to be touched. He'd called dibs, and in guy code that meant hands off. So why the hell were his best friend's hands all over her?

Toni finally looked up at him with a wink and a smile.

He imagined his fist smashing into his friend's face. That smile killed women—Destin had seen it. He loved the guy, and understood that flirting was like breathing to him, but he wanted Toni to get his hands off Nicole.

Nicole turned then and laid a daring look on Destin. She was rocking sensually from side to side. Toni's hands were on her hips, and that smile was on his face.

He was dead.

Thereza touched her hand to Destin's chin to get his attention. He nodded, trying not to be impolite, but twirled them around so he could see Nicole. Thereza turned and followed his gaze. Before he knew what was happening, Thereza broke out of his grasp, kicked her leg in the air, arched her back, swung her body down and slowly glided her ass up to run along Destin's thighs to his pelvis. Nicole watched, an unsure expression on her face. Her gaze met his. All he could do was shake his head and shrug.

Toni took that as a cue to spin Nicole around and bend her back into a low dip. Her hair came out of the bun in a seductive wave. Then, with the flick of his wrist, Toni snapped her back to his side and pulled her leg onto his hip. Her skirt shifted the black lace patterns, revealing the edge of red silk.

Destin's fists clenched. That was it. He flashed a look at Toni, and in a smooth, coordinated move, the men swapped women.

"You're welcome, brother!" Toni shouted.

"Shut up," Destin growled back.

Nicole was still getting her bearings. When she finally looked up, she bit her lip and grinned at Destin. A little shy. Very sexy.

Thereza hit Toni and stormed off. He rolled his eyes, flashed that smile and went after her.

"Looks like Toni isn't Thereza's type," Nicole said.

"I hope not. They're half brother and sister. Same father—long story." He looked into her eyes. "I'm sorry about your appointments."

Nicole's eyes softened. She nodded and began to pull back. Destin grabbed her waist and hauled her against him. "The song's not over."

He led her into a slow dance, his hands low on her hips, pulling her against him from thigh to chest. She smelled like vetiver and vanilla, and he resisted the urge to taste the silky skin of her neck.

He wanted to know how she'd gotten there, why the hell she was dancing with Toni, if she realized how dangerous it was to be in a favela by herself at such a late hour.

He should be angry that she'd seen his plans firsthand. The wines he'd hid from his father's company were flowing freely, and she'd met most of the investors in his new venture. If she made a phone call right now, she could ruin him.

He wasn't going to let her out of his sight.

And all the ways he could do that thrust his thoughts in a more intimate direction.

Chapter 17

The music pulsed through them, and they began a natural, slow sway, their bodies moving in unspoken unison. He watched her under lowered lids. His grip on her waist tightened, and she felt his hand slip a little lower.

Being wrapped in his arms again felt good.

It occurred to her that she should tell him about the offer from Clay, but she didn't want to ruin the moment.

Not yet.

She stared at his lips, noting the bottom one was fuller than the top, remembering how firm and smooth they were.

"Not bad." His voice was low, dark. "Here, follow me."

She'd never pegged him for a dancer, but before she knew was happening, Destin had spun her around, pulled her back against his chest and run his hand down the side of her body. His hips pressed into her bottom, guiding her into a seductive two-step.

"That's it," he breathed.

She did what she was told, leaning back against him, feeling bolder. His hand grazed the side of her breast, sending electricity down her spine.

Nicole backed it up into Destin, rolling and circling her hips, but just brushing the fabric of his pants. She was in the middle of a hip roll when he grabbed her and pulled her more firmly against him. She lost her step, but quickly recovered, grinding against him, all of him.

She'd made an assumption after they'd shared their first kiss at the château. Assumption confirmed. He was big everywhere.

His fingers curled into her hips, keeping her in one place. He bent to her ear. "You are trouble."

She spun around to face him. "Me? You're the one dirty dancing. Where did you learn this?"

He spun her around and pulled her back to his chest. "I've lived in Brazil for a very long time." He groaned at the way she slid against him. "What's your excuse?"

"I'm from Brooklyn." On instinct, Nicole turned around to face Destin, pulled his head down toward her and forced her mouth against his.

It wasn't supposed to be this good. The music and the kiss created a heady cocktail, paired with his rock-hard body. She let herself get lost in him. She molded her curves to his torso, feeling the strength of him through his shirt, wanting more than just a kiss.

Her hands skimmed up over his chest just as his fingers dug into her hair, and she rose on her toes when his hand stroked down her back. With a squeeze on her ass, he kissed her deeper, pulling her closer against him.

His mouth ate at hers. Somewhere in the back of her mind, she realized that they were no longer fighting their feelings. They had crossed into foreplay territory, which made the hard pounding of his heart feel so much sweeter.

But she knew him now, knew that at some point he'd

break it off and back away. He'd throw her job in her face and leave her stranded. She had to catch this feeling while she could, so she dug in and kissed him fiercely, holding on to him like her life depended on it.

She ran her fingertips over his beard and reveled in the subtle scratches against her cheeks. His kisses turned slow and deep, the kind that made girls' panties wriggle off on their own. She began to shamelessly rub herself against his insistent erection.

Destin pulled back, his erratic breathing blowing against her mouth. His lips were just inches from hers, but he didn't release her.

And she sure as hell wasn't moving.

The feel of her had him reeling, and after the song was over, he grabbed her hand and brought her to the side of the bar. Even now, as she stood at his shoulder waiting for her drink, close but not touching, he could sense her, wanted her tucked in beside him. He rubbed at his beard and fidgeted against the torturous pull.

Why was it that every time she touched him, he felt that he was going to spontaneously combust?

A small tasting bar was set up in the corner with some promotional bottles of wine. He plucked a bottle of wine and two glasses from the display then poured them both a glass. With a steadying breath, he turned to Nicole. Her skin was shining, and she had put her hair back up in a loose bun. She stopped fanning herself and reached for her glass.

His eyes strayed to the transparent, lacy parts of her dress when she took a sip. Taking her hand, he led them through the crowd, then up the stairs to a private lounge behind the DJ booth. Nicole made herself comfortable on the plush couch, crossing her legs in his direction. She caught him staring, but the salacious grin he gave her said he wasn't ashamed.

"So, this is what you were hiding," she said, her gaze running over the crowd below. "Why? So you want to crowdfund to bid on the land, big deal."

"This wine," he held up his glass, "and the batches in the cellar, are technically property of Dechamps France."

"I see. And the vines?"

Destin nodded. "My father could take those, too. I've declassified most of the wines you see here, bottling them just a smidge too early, with no label, but he could still legally take what's in the cask room as his. And I can't let that happen. My investors are in as long as we can start selling within the next six months."

"So you can sell and rebuild at the same time."

"Exactly."

"And what does Elliot think about this plan? He has a stake in the land, too."

"Elliot stands to make money regardless of who owns the land, but our father's claim to the wines will affect him indirectly. Like I said, I deliberately don't tell him everything I'm doing, but Anton knows, so I'm sure he knows more than he should."

She gave him a pointed look. "Anton! That's how you knew about my appointments." Destin smiled, glad she seemed more surprised than angry. "Oh, my God, I thought he was helping me." She frowned. "That's not cool."

"Maybe you've noticed, but Anton and my brother spend a lot of time together."

Her eyes narrowed. "I have noticed that, actually. When one was in the room, so was the other. And Elliot seemed to have a lot of 'business meetings' at the hotel." Her jaw dropped as realization dawned on her. "Oh, they're a cute couple."

Destin just smiled and sipped his wine. "My brother hasn't said a word, but it's obvious. And I think it's why Anton is helping me. If the land in Brazil is gone, Elliot may have to move back to France."

"Is that what you would do?"

His eyes narrowed. "I'm not losing the land."

"Well, I'm not, either."

Destin raised one eyebrow. "Does that mean you're going to tell on me?"

"No, but I'm drawing a line in the sand. No more sabotage. If you want the land, you outbid everyone else. Deal?"

"Is this how you treat all your clients?"

"Only the unruly ones."

"Okay, Miss Parks," he said, leaning closer to run a finger over her cheek. "You have a deal."

"That's what I like to hear." She moved her body inches from his. "But no more shop talk. This is a party. I'm not always all work, you know."

He feigned shock and tipped his wine down his throat. "Oh yeah?" He moved closer. "Prove it."

Nicole smiled seductively against his lips just as alarm bells sounded and the music stopped. The counter was flashing a little over two hundred thousand dollars. Toni waved at Destin and beckoned him to the DJ booth. Destin leaned in and kissed Nicole full on the mouth. "I'll be right back."

Nicole stood and walked to the railing for a better look. Destin took the microphone and began to speak in Portuguese. The crowd clapped and whistled, and after a few minutes they erupted into a harmonious roar.

She clapped, too, letting pride well up in her chest. She had always known the winery wasn't just a vanity project for Destin, but seeing the people's support below showed her that he would, indeed, be giving something back to this community. A lot more than a casino would.

"I don't know what you said, but it sounded awesome," she said when Destin returned.

"I just thanked everyone because with their help we are closer to our goal. Just a little more time and I can move forward."

"What does moving forward look like?"

"Like this." He wrapped her in his arms and brushed a kiss over her lips.

"Destin, after what I've seen here tonight, the strides you've made and the support you have—I need you to know that I won't get in your way." The statement came out before she'd even thought about it.

He looked concerned. "What does that mean?"

"It means," she said, her heart racing, "I'll quit. It will take your father a minute to find another broker, and that should give you enough time to make your bid."

He blinked. "You'd do that? What about your promotion?"

She thought of the adoption agency. "Maybe it wasn't meant to be," she murmured.

"No. You're not quitting. I need you here. I'm ready to talk to my father. That's why my friends are here. We're getting investment paperwork ready and making the bid in a few days. I need a broker."

Her eyes widened. "I can't work for your father and you at the same time. I really think I should quit—"

He cut her off with a kiss. "Don't do anything yet." He stared into her eyes. "I mean it, Nicole."

"Okay." She nodded, holding onto Destin. Wondering how she was going to deal with Clay and the offer she'd already forwarded to Elliot.

The fundraising might have been over, but the party was just beginning. Wine flowed, the DJ spun hard beats and the dancing didn't stop. She had no idea how many drinks she'd had, but when she stopped moving, the room continued to spin.

"Nicole, are you okay?" Destin's concerned voice was close to her ear. He hadn't left her side since he'd spotted her dancing with Toni.

"Um… I think I just need some water."

"Did you eat?"

"A little at the hotel."

"Come. I'm taking you for food."

Leaving the warehouse happened in a blur. Someone hugged her. Destin was saying goodbye to somebody, his hand steady around hers. Where in the world were they going to get food at two in the morning? Moments later, Nicole was seated in the Jeep, thankful for the cool wind in her face. Destin's hand was on her thigh, holding her in place.

"You look a little green, *chérie*."

The French endearment made her smile, but her stomach quickly turned. How did she end up having so much to drink? Toni and that damn cachaça.

They parked at the docks, and Destin helped her out of the Jeep, keeping a steady arm around her as they walked toward the beach. They walked over a little wooden walkway that descended to the sand.

"I thought we were getting food."

"We are." Destin stopped and leaned them against the wooden railing. "The *pescador* are out. Fishermen," he said, giving her a quick kiss before he bent in front of her and held out his hands. "Shoes."

With a good grip on the railing, she lifted her right foot. He looked into her eyes and caressed her calf before slipping off her shoe.

"This feels familiar," she said, lifting her other foot. "Those shoes better be intact when I get them back."

Destin half smiled. "I'll guard them with my life."

He shucked his own shoes and socks, and rolled up his pants legs. Their shoes in his hands, he held out his elbow for her, and they walked along the darkened shore.

Fishing boats and their tiny lights bobbed up and down on the black sea, while several fishermen were already unloading their cargo on the beach. Nicole saw a string of lights a short distance away, then noticed the beachside bar they were strung on.

"Welcome to my favorite place." Destin held open a skinny door for her, and she stepped in, feeling conscious of her bare feet. She didn't need to be. Everyone in the dimly lit place was either barefoot or half naked, and most were men. "This is where the real men hang out," Destin said with a wink.

Fishermen, farmers and factory workers, some working overnight, some up before dawn, were all digging into plates filled with delicious-smelling food. A busty, middle-aged redhead came out from the kitchen when she saw Destin and kissed him on both cheeks. She pointed toward the back, and they slid next to each other in a corner booth. With a smile, the redhead slapped some menus and a tea light on the table.

"Mona keeps this place open for the invisibles."

"Invisibles?"

"People who are working while everyone is sleeping. Mona's husband has been a fisherman for over forty years."

"You're an invisible?"

"I've been here many mornings after harvest."

"You're not invisible. I see you."

He took her hand and ran the back of his fingers over her cheek. "I see you, too."

"I like this playful mood you're in. It's better than your angry lecture mood," Nicole teased.

He laughed, leaning closer. "I'm feeling…hopeful. Like anything is possible."

Nicole frowned, her thoughts again shifting to Clay's offer. She had to talk to Elliot.

"What's going through your head?" Destin smoothed a lock of hair out of her face.

"Um, I was just wondering what *vin amante* meant. It sounds French, but isn't."

"It's a mash-up. The French *vin*, meaning wine, and Portuguese *amante*, meaning lover. Wine lover."

"Oh." She nodded. "It's you."

"It's us," he breathed, placing a lingering kiss on her lips.

Mona brought out a large plate of meats, fresh fish pieces and fried oysters. They dug in with their hands. The simple fare was grilled to perfection and accented with crisp fruits and vegetables.

Destin ate steadily, popping bites into his mouth and feeding her the morsels he liked best. Nicole's stomach stopped turning, and she nestled in the crook of his arm when she felt her eyelids droop.

"Come," Destin said into her hair. "I'll take you to your hotel."

She shook her head. She was warm and fed, and Destin's arm around her shoulders felt so good. She relaxed into him, letting her eyelids close for just a second.

"Nicole?"

Destin's kiss in her hair was the last thing she remembered.

Chapter 18

With every step back to the Jeep, Destin felt a tug of reluctance. Their night was ending, as was their time together. Soon the land would be his, and she'd be gone.

Nicole climbed into the front and fastened her seatbelt, resting her head against the leather seat, gazing out at the moonlit ocean. Destin jumped in and started the Jeep. Nicole stifled a yawn.

"Back to your hotel, young lady. I think you're done for the night." He made a mental note to pick her car up from the lot tomorrow.

"Mmm. It was a good night. Thank you."

Destin caught her gaze. Those dark eyes were glassy and a little unfocused. He cupped her cheek and kissed her gently, leaning in more at her passionate response. The clutch of her hand on his shirt brought him closer.

He pulled back deliberately, fighting his baser instincts to kidnap her, take her back to his château and make love to her until sunrise. But she was tired and a little drunk. He didn't want this night to be something she regretted.

Destin started the Jeep and accelerated out into the street, smiling to himself when she shook out her hair in the breeze. He remembered the feel of her grinding against him, the sexy curve of her lower back and the full softness of her lips. They'd moved like lovers. And had they really been lovers, he would take her home and make sure she knew she was his.

His body heated at the thought of kissing her all over. If only things were different.

By the end of the week, he'd have the land. He could feel it. But where did that leave Nicole? To draw up paperwork and go back to New York? That sinking feeling washed over him again.

Destin glanced at Nicole, who was fighting to keep her eyes open. What could he do to make her stay just a little longer?

That last thought lingered as he rolled to a stop in front of the hotel.

"Nicole," he whispered, running the back of his finger over her cheek. Her head lolled toward him, and her eyes fluttered closed. "It's time to get you to bed."

"Mmmmm…" she murmured into her shoulder.

His gaze shifted to the lobby where a lone attendant was working. He could carry her to her room, but someone would have to let him in, which would involve a lot of explaining he wasn't interested in doing.

Nicole jerked awake when they parked in front of Destin's château. She focused for a second on the house, then her lids dropped and her head relaxed again.

"Nicole, we're home."

"Okay." She didn't move.

Destin came around to her side of the Jeep, unbuckled her seat belt and slid her forward so he could pick her up.

She woke then, putting her hands on his shoulders and sliding out of the car. Destin held onto her waist as she found her footing.

"Kiss me," she said in a tiny voice.

He smiled and did what he was told, then kept a hand on her as she navigated the short distance to the door. Quickly, Destin shoved the key into the lock and slapped on the lights as Nicole shuffled inside, kicking her shoes off in the foyer. Where was her purse?

Leaving the door open, Destin ran back to the Jeep and found the little clutch on the floor.

"Magnus, you're amazing!" He heard Nicole's squeal of delight as he entered the foyer and closed the door. He placed her purse on the counter and found her in the living room, lying facedown on the couch, her dress askew. Magnus was sniffing rapidly, probably making sure she was still alive.

Destin hurried to the guest room and turned down the duvet, then he walked back to the couch.

"Roll over, baby. I'm putting you to bed."

She didn't move. He turned her around and lifted her in his arms, grinning as she murmured unintelligible things under her breath. Her eyes were slits, and he felt an urgency to get her comfortable. She needed to sleep.

He carried her to the guest room and laid her down, smoothing her hair back from her face. He reached for the bedside lamp, then stopped, unable to look away from her parted lips or her body's curves on top of the soft sheets.

He fought the urge to crawl in beside her and pull her into his arms. Instead, he reached for the blanket and gently covered her, then clicked off the little light. Afraid she'd have a killer headache when she woke, he fetched her a glass of water and carefully placed it on the nightstand along with two aspirin.

The door widened, and Magnus came in and sank down on the rug beside the bed.

"No, Magnus. Let's go," Destin whispered.

The dog placed his head on his paws and ignored him. Destin nudged him with his foot, but the dog didn't move. "Magnus." Destin sighed, speaking a little louder and softly slapping his thigh. "Magnus."

"Destin?" The voice that rose from the bed was soft and sultry.

"Sorry. It's just Magnus and me. Go back to sleep."

"Come here." She half rose from the duvet and reached for him. She caught his hand, and with surprising strength she pulled him closer—or was it that he was already moving in her direction? His eyes had yet to adjust, but he could feel her hands on his arms and then her lips on his. His resolve melted with every taste of her mouth and every stroke of her tongue.

The duvet fell away, and her movements tugged her dress down, revealing more of her tantalizing shoulders. He needed her naked, yet he stopped himself, mentally torn between instinct and his conscience.

Better judgment said she might still be drunk. Instinct said he should get her out of that stifling dress. Her needy moan broke his thought. She was wine and heat, woman and goddess. He couldn't resist. But he had to.

He placed a knee on the bed. His palms found her shoulders, and he broke off their kiss to gently push her back down to the bed. He pulled the duvet up to her chin.

She let out a frustrated sigh, which mirrored his own feelings.

"I want you," she said.

"I want you, too. But not like this."

"Like what? I'm not drunk."

"You're not sober, either. And you can barely keep your eyes open."

"Then keep me awake."

He'd love to. "Sleep. This," he leaned over and gave her a lingering kiss, "will still be here in the morning."

"But it will be different. Tomorrow is always different." The last words trailed off into a murmur as her eyes drifted shut.

Slowly, he slid off the bed. She was right. The saying was "seize the day," not "seize tomorrow morning."

He looked at Magnus, who yawned and stretched, making himself even more comfortable. *Fine. One of us might as well sleep with her.*

Destin stalked, angry and frustrated, to his bedroom. He whipped open his bay window, inviting the cool breeze, and cursed the full moon. *No wonder*, he thought. A full moon made people crazy. When he'd turned down Nicole just now, he'd clearly lost his mind. He shrugged out of his clothes, climbed naked into bed and stared at the glowing orb.

Destin had no idea how long he'd been asleep. He came awake when the bed dipped. Nicole sat on the edge of it beside him, her hair teasing her bare shoulders and her lips glistening in the moonlight. Her eyes were focused, and her gaze ran a path over his naked torso, then lower to where the sheet tangled on his hips. He half rose and propped himself on his elbow, securing the sheet at his waist.

"Nicole," he said, his voice like gravel. "Are you okay?"

"No, I can't get out of this dress." She turned and brushed her hair back. The zipper was halfway down and stuck, but all he could focus on was the silken expanse of her back.

"Here, let me help you." Her skin glistened, and he couldn't help but smooth his fingertips down her spine and over her thick bra strap. It was the lightest touch that had her turning her head to the side. Ending his exploration, he tugged the zipper a few times before working it free, then he pulled it all the way down to the stopper.

The dress gaped open, giving him an eyeful of her lower back and a glimpse of lacy red panties. What would she do if he kissed her there?

"Thank you," she said into the dark, relief in her voice. He stared at her movements as she began to peel her arms from the dress; the hourglass shape of her held him enthralled. Again, her head turned to the side.

"Could you unsnap me?" Her voice turned dark, sexy. His body reacted in kind, and he loosened his bed sheet.

He swallowed hard. "Sure." The word could barely be heard. He tried with one hand, but the little hooks on her bra were tougher than they looked. He sat up fully, his cover dangerously low, and used both of his hands to free her.

"Thank you." She stood and turned, holding his gaze as she clenched the dress and bra to her breast. Without breaking eye contact, she let them both fall to her waist, then bent to shove the dress down her hips. Her breasts swayed forward as she worked the fabric down, letting it slide to the floor.

Riveted, Destin watched her step out of the pool of black lace at her feet and step into the moonlight that slashed the room. Her red panties glowed against her dark skin, beckoning him to touch.

He didn't dare blink. She looked ethereal standing before him, nude and perfect, her nipples diamond hard. She could have been Hathor, the Egyptian Goddess of Love and Beauty, or a mythical siren of the sea, come to use him for her pleasure. He'd be taken, gladly.

Destin eased his legs over the edge of the bed to sit, allowing the sheet to completely slide free. He was erect, and getting more so as the dark challenge in her eyes shifted lower. Nicole. Did she know it was a French name, and that it meant *victorious*?

And he felt victorious, because he would no longer deny himself what he wanted so badly.

"Come toward me." It wasn't a request; it was a command. Destin's navy gaze caressed her breasts, her torso, and her thighs and the pulsing apex in between. She simply stood, relishing the sight of his taut muscles and smooth skin, in awe of the power that rose between his legs. "Come here, Nicole," he repeated, impatient.

She bit her lip and studied his smoldering gaze, relishing her power over him. Slowly she walked forward. Who was she kidding? He had power over her, too.

When she got within arm's length, he reached for her, pulling her close until she stood just inside his open thighs. She quivered at his touch, and his ragged breath told her he was feeling the same uncontrollable desire.

"I can't stop this time, Nicole. I won't stop." He placed a light kiss on her pelvis, just above her panties, and ran his hands up the backs of her thighs to her bottom. He sank his fingers under her panties, into her flesh, and groaned.

She dug her fingers into his hair and looked into his smoldering gaze. "I don't want you to stop."

"You are incredible," Destin said, accenting his words with another squeeze, worship in his voice. Sliding his fingers to her sides, he slid her panties over her hips and down her thighs to her calves, steadying her as she lifted one leg, then the other. In a bold move, he scrunched the fabric in his hand, brought it to his face and inhaled.

Her lips parted as lust shot down her spine, making her ache and throb between her legs.

"Like wine, I knew it," he gritted out, letting the panties fall to the floor. "Spread your legs."

He teased her with his fingers first, probing, exploring,

his gaze repeatedly flicking to hers to gauge her reaction.
She stood still, her breathing shallow, her lids fluttering
against the onslaught of sensation.

Her breath caught at the first slick glide of his tongue.
His moan ended on a sigh, and her hips surged forward,
reaching for him when he pulled back. His palms grabbed
her hips and held her in place as he reached for her again,
tasting and teasing, nipping and sucking, tormenting her
as she got closer and closer to the edge.

Her eyes drifted shut, and she let out a moan before his
name drifted from her lips into the darkness.

"Destin…" she panted.

"Stay with me." As if she'd go anywhere.

Her eyes flew open when he lifted her onto the bed.
He eased up her body. Shifting so she didn't take his full
weight, he kissed her fully, thoroughly, consuming her as
if he were dying of thirst, and she was water and wine.
Her body undulated under his and her fingers locked in
his hair. His lips found her shoulder, her throat and the
swell of her breasts.

Her nipple tingled under the warmth of his breath and
the tickle of his beard. She moaned when he took her fully
into his mouth and then transferred his attentions to the
other breast. She arched under him, begging for the velvet smoothness of his tongue.

Destin shifted again and came back to take her lips in
a series of slow, soft kisses. Her pulse hammered and her
body felt like a battery, charged and ready. Gripping his
back, she wound her legs around his waist in invitation.
He broke their kiss and smiled, a wicked, devilish smile
that had her blood thickening in her veins. Without letting
go of her, he reached into the nightstand for a condom,
took her mouth in a kiss, then drove himself inside of her
with a series of measured, rhythmic thrusts that had her
breaking his kiss and whispering his name.

She'd never made love like this. Never. He drove himself deep, growling low in his throat, rocking her into the bed. She couldn't think, gasped for breath in her lungs, was overwhelmed by the thick, heavy feel of him, and the relentless, unyielding surge of his hips. She wanted to stay there forever.

Another moan ripped from her throat, and her body trembled under his. He shifted, releasing her mouth, staring down at her, his breathing harsher. He was close. She was, too; her nipples ached against his chest. She felt his rhythm shift, felt the increased passion of his kiss. He slid his hand under her and pulled her up to meet him. It was dizzying—every stroke brought her closer, every thrust took her higher.

"Look at me," he grunted.

Her cloudy gaze caught his. Their pleasure built, then burst. He gripped her, and she him. Her body shook around him, stretched taut, then finally released. Destin pumped furiously, his arms locked around her, kissing her through every wave of their simultaneous climax.

Nicole lay awake under the luxurious sheet, warm and contently tucked into the crook of Destin's arm. He slept on his back, his breathing silent, and the rise and fall of his chest was slight and even.

Her body was still humming. Maybe that was why she couldn't sleep. No, that wasn't it. Clay's words were haunting her. *Nobody wants it more than me.* Clay was her sure thing when she was out to sell the land, but now her feelings had changed.

She'd been a lawyer long enough to know that family business disputes were rarely just about business; they were about sorting out old issues of rivalry and dominance. If Destin and his father were locked in a room for twenty-four hours, would this rift go away? Could Destin keep what was rightfully his? The ceiling had provided no answers.

"Hey." He propped himself on his elbow and captured her lips in a soft kiss. "You're awake."

"Can't sleep."

He deepened the kiss, his thumb grazing her jawline and his thigh slipping between her legs to get closer. He broke the kiss and studied her face. "Everything okay?"

She nodded but lowered her head, afraid he'd see her thoughts.

He softly lifted her chin with his knuckle. "Are you having regrets?"

"No. God no." She snuggled closer.

"Then what?"

She opened her mouth but nothing would come out. His hands came around her face and he rolled up to kiss her again. "The moonlight can be blinding. I'll close the curtain if—"

"That's not it," she whispered. He caressed her cheek, waiting patiently, his eyes imploring her to trust him. "What if you and your father talked things—"

With an exasperated, sigh, Destin rolled onto his back. "It won't help, Nicole. I've tried so many times. Once my mother passed away he became a tyrant. Really, the only person that could talk to him after that was…" he paused "… Nina."

Destin was blinking up at the ceiling, the moon outlining a stoic look on his face. He was thinking of the fire.

Nicole swallowed. "Destin…what happened?" He was silent for a long moment. "I'm sorry. It's none of my business." There was more silence, and then he began to speak.

"We had a break-in in the main house. Nina kept oil lamps in each room. We used them for power outages mostly, but she would light one for me in the foyer by the door when I worked after dark. I had fallen asleep on the couch in the cellar. Magnus was barking when I woke. I remember thinking he must have seen a rabbit, he was so excited. When I opened the door, the house was engulfed in flames."

Nicole stayed silent, but her heart beat in her ears as he continued in a low whisper.

"I ran around the front and the back, trying to find a space to get in. I broke through a side window and ran to the bedroom." His voice caught. "I was too late. The police had conducted an investigation and concluded a lamp had been knocked over. There seemed to be evidence that someone tried to put it out, but they couldn't find any leads on the intruder."

Nicole swiped at a few tears. "Oh my God, I'm so sorry."

Destin rolled up onto his elbow and cupped her face. "Please don't cry."

"I shouldn't have asked."

"No, I'm glad you did," he said into her eyes. "I think I've been wanting to share that with you. It's not something I talk about, but I wanted you to know. It says something."

"What does it say?"

"That maybe I'm not dead inside like I thought I was. I will always love Nina, but I'm ready to have a life again. You've brought me out of a living coma."

Destin kissed her tears as she tried to get control of her emotions. They held on to each other for a long moment, kissing and touching.

"Thank you for sharing that with me," Nicole said.

Destin brushed her tousled hair from her face. "I've been thinking. Back at the château when I asked you about children, I made you upset. I wondered what that was about."

She blinked, suddenly feeling defective. "I told you, you can't always have everything you want—that's life."

"I'm not judging you, Nicole."

She took a deep breath. He'd bared his soul and now she was crawling back into her shell? No, he deserved an answer.

"I know that." Her voice calmed. "Actually, I've been in the process of adopting a child. I'd like a daughter. It's been hard because they have all of these rules, which become even more important when you are single." The word turned to ice on her tongue. "Financial stability, a home with a room for the child, access to a nanny, etc. And it can take years for a family to pick you. Everything has to look perfect on paper. Right now, I don't look perfect. A one-bedroom apartment, with no man and no parents, doesn't scream stable home."

"You look perfect to me," he said, his gaze softened. "And I think you'd make a good mother. You're strong." More tears came so quick, she was embarrassed to let him see, but he wouldn't let her pull away.

No one had ever said such beautiful things to her before. No one. He held her for a long moment, placing kisses in her hair. Nicole's head came up and she gently pushed him onto his back. "Destin, I…" His hand came up to her face. And she lost her nerve. "Make love to me again."

In one powerful motion, he smoothed a hand under her bottom and lifted her over his body. They both moaned when she eased slowly down onto him. "Destin," she whispered over him…

Chapter 19

Destin woke to find himself awash in the hot Brazilian sunlight, caught in a tangle of sheets and Nicole's gorgeous limbs. He didn't need a watch to know it was late morning. Nicole's breathing was even on his chest, and he shifted his head to gaze at her sleeping form. She must be exhausted, he thought. He smiled. He was, too, and yet as he gazed at her long exposed legs, he debated kissing her awake and hitching those legs on his back until well into the afternoon.

No, she needed to sleep. He raised his eyebrow and grinned. It would give her a fighting chance against him later. Carefully slipping out from under her, he rolled from the bed and closed the curtains. Turning, he saw Magnus in the doorway, ready and waiting for his breakfast.

Destin tossed on his lounge pants, gently closed the bedroom door and shuffled into the kitchen. Magnus's kibble pounded into the metal bowl and set off a hammering in Destin's temples. He needed to crawl back into bed with his woman.

They'd crossed a threshold last night. Shared things. They'd been intimate, in more ways than one. He wanted to know more about her, wanted to know everything.

He poured water into Magnus's other bowl, then downed a glass himself. All he could taste was her. They'd made love in multiple positions until morning, and the images were burned into his psyche. He was getting turned on just thinking about it. That's all it took. A single thought.

Destin turned toward the bedroom, but stopped when he heard a loud knock on the door. Magnus let out a gruff bark.

"Destin?" came his brother's muffled voice.

What was he doing here? Destin glanced at the bedroom door, debating whether to let Elliot in. Another knock.

"Destin, we're coming in."

We? Suddenly a key was shoved into the lock. The only other person who had keys was…*merde*! Destin walked to the foyer and watched in horror as his father's small, yet formidable form came through the door. The cane Armand carried held the gold Dechamps crest. Elliot's lean frame followed, mouthing an apology over their father's head.

"You didn't answer the door," his father said in his signature monotone. Armand stopped and leaned on his cane, his focus on the women's shoes in the middle of the foyer. His silver head swiveled up to Destin's half-dressed body, and he let out a heavy sigh of exasperation.

"*Bonjour* Father. Elliot." Destin followed them into the living room and placed himself so he could keep an eye on the bedroom door.

Elliot stood next to his father. His gaze swung from the

women's heels to the closed bedroom door. Destin met Elliot's knowing look with his own defiant stare.

Nicole could wake at any moment. He had to get them out of there.

"You're still sleeping," Armand cleared his throat. "Have we disturbed you?"

"Surprised me, more like. It's good to see you, of course. But whatever this is, can it wait till later?"

"We've accepted an offer. Our agent, Miss Parks, was quite industrious in securing a generous offer from The Texas Casino company. I've spoken to Mr. Winchester, and we've agreed to close in thirty days."

Destin's heart stopped. His gaze slid to Elliot, who was staring at him with genuine concern as his father rattled on.

"We are meeting as a board tomorrow at noon to properly vote and sign the paperwork so Miss Parks can begin finishing the deal. I have yet to meet her in person, but Elliot speaks quite highly. Have you met her?"

Destin swallowed, trying to find his voice. "Yes."

"Good. Tomorrow, then. We can discuss your coming back to France, then, as well."

Destin froze, swallowing the urge to raise his voice. "You said you'd give me time."

"You've had time. I can wait no longer."

"Thirty million." Destin was clumsy in his delivery, he knew, but he was having trouble keeping his cool.

"Not good enough."

"Thirty-five!" He didn't have it, but he'd get it. Somehow.

"The casino is at sixty."

Destin's mouth dropped and the oxygen seemed to leave his lungs. That was over the asking price. "I'm your son!"

"And you should be running our winery in France!" Armand smacked his cane on the floor for emphasis. Then he composed himself and continued in an even tone. "To-morrow we will finish this."

"You don't need my vote. You have control."

"Yes, but I want your concession, in case you decide to sue me again."

His father's cane struck the kitchen floor as he hurried out. "And if you don't show, consider yourself fired from the board. The deal can still go through without you. And Destin—" His father turned back around. "Tomorrow we will discuss the cellar."

Destin couldn't think of anything to say. He couldn't think at all.

Elliot came forward and grabbed his shoulders, murmuring so their father couldn't hear. "I'm sorry. I tried. Have Nicole call me when she wakes."

"She said they hadn't made an offer," he whispered.

"It wasn't a formal offer, they were still in negotiations. There was a number but it was contingent upon seeing the wine cellar. But when Mr. Winchester couldn't get a hold of Nicole last night, he called Father directly. Father was already in Brazil. That's all I know so far. Make sure she calls me."

The door closed and Destin sank to the couch, his elbows propped on his knees as he held his head. Magnus curled up close to his foot. What had happened?

The bedroom door opened slowly. He didn't look up, only listened as Nicole padded into the living room. He studied the floor and clenched his fists, determined to control the growing wave of anger. Had she lied to him?

Nicole stood in his peripheral vision, barefoot with a sheet clutched to her naked breasts. He was afraid to look at her, especially since his body was already responding to her presence.

"I assume you heard. When were you going to tell me

they had made an offer?" His voice was even and cold. So much like his father's that it chilled him.

"Destin, it's not that simple. I've been back and forth with Clay for days. He lowballed and now he is dangling a high bid with a contingency, just to get us to bend when he pulls away. I've seen it before. And I told you that Clay wanted to see what was in the cellar before making a formal offer. I don't know what changed."

She moved forward to touch his shoulder. He rose quickly and faced her from across the room.

"When did the offer come through?"

"This last offer must have come through yesterday while I was…when we were…"

"You should have told me all of this."

Her eyes were wide, pleading. He forced his gaze to drift past her.

"This isn't over yet, Destin—no paperwork has been signed." She moved toward him. "Why won't you look at me?"

He did look at her then. There in front of him was a woman whose body he knew intimately, but who, in reality, he didn't know at all.

"Did you keep this from me on purpose?" he murmured.

"Of course not. What are you saying?"

"You'll definitely get your promotion now, right?"

She blinked. "That's not fair. You told me to do my job. That's what I did."

"Touché." His heart beat faster. He felt humiliated and betrayed…and empty. This whole plan had been his idea, he knew, but he felt like he was the one being played. She was a lawyer. Never trust a lawyer. When would he learn?

We'll talk about the cellar tomorrow. His father's words floated into his mind. What did he mean by that? Could he know about the wine?

Suddenly Destin had to get to the winery.

He bolted for the bedroom, trying to pull his thoughts together as he dragged on a T-shirt and jeans. He felt like he was losing everything at once. His land, the wine… Nicole.

"Destin, I'm so sorry." Nicole stood in the bedroom doorway.

"I have to go," he said in a detached voice.

She didn't plead with him to stay, just stood there watching him with a somber gaze. He was at the door when he turned back to her. "I almost forgot." Hope filled her eyes. "Elliot wants you to call him." He left before he could see her reaction.

Fifteen minutes later Destin was running across the property toward the cellar door, which was ajar. Two Brazilian men with a box of tools were just leaving. Carefully, he descended the stairs and winced when he found his father standing in the cask room. Elliot was at the wall playing with the temperature pad.

First they barge into his home, now his cellar? Destin let his anger rise to the surface then. "Get out!"

Elliot stepped away from the wall and stilled. Armand turned to Destin.

"You didn't think I believed you when you told me you dumped the casks, did you, son? I know you better than that. You'd cut off your arm first." Armand tapped his cane on a light oak barrel. "They must be close to maturation."

Destin clenched his fists, steeling himself against what he knew would happen next. He and his father had gone through this before. Destin had lost then, too. "So, what now, Father? You take it all back with you? If that's the case, I'll dump it the minute you leave."

"I wouldn't do that if I were you. You see, I promised Mr. Winchester that he could have whatever was in the cellar, including the wines, which he could market exclusively as his at the casino." Destin opened his mouth to protest, but his father held up a hand. "Since these wines are property of Dechamps, LLC, I have the right to do that."

Destin felt like a bullet had hit his gut. His wines, at a casino. Incredulous, Destin looked to Elliot, who slowly shook his head. Betrayed, by both his brother and Nicole. The sense of loss Destin felt was overwhelming. He thought of Nina, the one who had stood by him in everything. Then Nicole came into his mind. Gone. It was all gone.

Elliot rushed forward. "Destin, I know this is a shock. Let's talk upstairs."

The two men left their father in the cask room and took the stairs above ground.

"I know what you're thinking," Elliot started when they emerged from the cellar. "But I had no idea. He showed up this morning. I had to hide Anton in the closet."

Destin's gaze flicked to his brother's. He'd always suspected something was going on between them, but Elliot never spoke of his love life to him. His brother had basically just come out. He wished he was in a state of mind to celebrate that.

"In the closet, Destin. Ironic? Anton will probably never speak to me again after this," Elliot murmured. "Father told me he'd spoken to Mr. Winchester himself. It seems that when Mr. Winchester couldn't get a hold of Nicole, or me, he found Father."

Elliot raised a brow. "Can I assume Nicole was hiding in your closet this morning? I recognized her shoes from the first night at dinner. She has great shoes."

Destin stared at his brother for a long moment, then nodded. "I don't want to talk about Nicole. I need to figure out how to stop this." He began to pace.

Elliot sighed. "Destin, I told you to go to France and work this out with Father. You stayed here. Why?"

"I was getting the money together!"

"Is that the only reason?"

Destin stopped. "What are you saying?"

"She's remarkable, isn't she? I was there when you first met. I saw it at dinner."

"What are you talking about?" Destin asked, irritated.

"Amour," Elliot simply said.

"I didn't stay here for a woman, especially one who doesn't live here. This. Is. My. Home!" He wanted to hit something.

"Destin, I will say this to you for the last time. Let this go and move forward with your life. The land was never ours. We made a mistake entering a deal with the most ruthless man in the world—our own father. Give him what he wants and build something new." Elliot stepped closer with a pointed look. "Maybe you can start fresh with someone else by your side?"

Let it go? Destin stepped back, feeling like the foundation under his feet was crumbling. Why could he trust no one around him?

With a blunt goodbye, Destin left his brother and drove back to the château. He walked straight to the bedroom, but only Magnus was present, sniffing and wandering. Looking for her, too. Not a trace of Nicole was there. He was relieved—and yet the tug at his heart said otherwise.

He stared at the crumpled sheets, feeling like he'd lost something vital. A part of himself. Something that might have been the thing he needed most in the world. Because he knew that whatever had been between him and Nicole...*amour*?...was now over.

That night, Destin knocked softly on his father's hotel room door, trying to ignore the fact that Nicole's room was only two floors up. He couldn't get the last image of her out of his mind. Bare feet and shoulders, with his sheet wrapped under her arms. He hadn't given her a chance to explain. Hell, he wouldn't have listened if she had tried.

His father opened the door, surprise registering briefly on his face before that stern countenance settled back in.

"What is it, Destin?"

"I'd like to talk."

Armand stepped away from the door, and Destin entered, his gaze sweeping the high ceilings of the luxury suite.

"Drink?" His father poured himself a whiskey.

"No, *merci.*" Destin sat on the couch, thinking about how to start. His father took his drink and settled in the chair at the large business desk across the room. A passive-aggressive sign of who was in charge. Destin sighed. Why did he even try?

"Forgive the distance, but I cannot sit on those couches. I'm an old man, Destin."

It scared him to know that was true. Fair enough. Destin rose from the couch and sat in one of the desk chairs, thinking it was fitting, as their relationship had always been more business than family.

"So, you've finally come to see me."

"I'm begging you to reconsider."

His father's gaze didn't waver. "I can't."

"Why? The real reason. Not this shit about needing money."

"We do need money, Destin. Now, not in five years."

"Who is we?"

"You and me. Like I said, I'm an old man. And you have always been my successor, whether you wanted to be or not."

Destin looked away and picked at his cuticles. "I wanted it once."

"Before Nina."

"Before you legally stole my wines." Destin struggled to keep his voice calm.

The men locked gazes. His father looked away first.

"That was regrettable. It never should have gotten that far. I let my pride get in the way of our family. I apologize."

Did hell just freeze over? His father had apologized. Destin took a good look at his father. He was frail and thin, and the tumbler of whiskey he put to his lips was shaking slightly.

"Mother wanted Elliot and me to have the land. It was hers first."

His father's blue gaze snapped up, and Destin recalled his mother's observation. *You have your father's eyes.*

"Your mother and I built this company. But there will be nothing left if we do not sell this land."

Destin sat forward. "What's going on?"

"I've made some decisions that haven't fared well for our company. We are broke. Our debts are mounting, and if we don't pay them, someone else will. And then they will own Dechamps, not us."

"I'm tired of hearing about your financial mistakes."

"It's more than that." Armand's hand quivered as he laid it across his mouth. Destin had never seen his father so shaken.

"What in God's name are you talking about?"

Armand drained his whiskey. "I can no longer hold on to this secret. It's killing me from the inside out." Armand let out a long exhale. "After our dispute, you refused to tell me what labels you were making. And when our financier found out you were declassifying our wines to sell them direct to consumers, they were furious. It was agreed that they would send someone to break into the winery and find out what you were doing. The fire was an accident."

Destin froze, blinking his way through a haze of anger and confusion.

"Destin. My son. I'm… I'm so sorry. Nina was fantastic. She was—"

"Don't talk about her!" Destin rose from his seat. He towered over his father. His fists hammered the desk. "You knew this whole time. I racked my brain thinking I did something to cause her death. That maybe, had I not been in the cellar that night, I could have saved her. There were nights I wished that I had died with her." His raised voice cracked.

"Son, don't say that." Armand's face was stricken at the thought of how close his son had come to dying.

"But you knew," said Destin, his tone harsh. "You let them invade my home."

"I didn't know until it was too late to stop it." Armand's voice was barely a whisper.

Destin backed away slowly, watching as Armand's shoulders began to shake, and tears fell to the desktop.

"How could you keep this from me?" Destin whispered.

"Son, please…" Armand stood but lost his grip and sank back to the chair.

"No! I'm done, Father. I have nothing left."

Destin left the room at once and stood by the elevators, his finger hovering over the up button. *Talk to her.* His hand shook, then he took long strides to the stairs.

He was in the lobby and outside the entrance in record time.

Chapter 20

The next morning, Nicole reached the hotel conference room early and waited for the arrival of Elliot, Armand and Destin. It was a quick premeeting to review Clay's offer and the next steps in the process. It was also a way for her to redeem herself. The slew of missed calls and emails regarding Clay's final offer had been embarrassing, as was the excuse she'd given Gustavo. She couldn't tell her boss she'd been drinking, dancing and making love with their client all night.

Ugh! She held her head in her hands. She loved him. She was an idiot.

Her only hope was that the meeting would go quickly and any interaction she had with Destin would be painless. Last night she had pried Destin's number from Anton and called him. When he didn't pick up, she'd texted. Nothing. She could take a hint. And, sadly, she understood. He'd been devastated. He'd been hurt. And she had facilitated that.

The paperwork she had drawn up today would vanquish the one thing he cared about the most. She'd actually cried a little when she printed out the stacks that lay on the table for them. She'd gained her sale, and now could go back home and go after the life she wanted.

The feelings she had for Destin were real, but it was never meant to be. His life was here. Hers was in New York. Regardless of who got the land, they were never going to be together.

And those thoughts alone made her feel lost and a little hopeless.

Elliot and Monsieur Dechamps arrived together, with Elliot making introductions.

"*Enchanté*, Ms. Parks. Thank you for bringing us to this point today. Elliot says you are brilliant." Armand kissed Nicole on both cheeks, and his smile touched his blue eyes. Destin's eyes.

"It's been a pleasure. I'm glad I've been able to be helpful." She handed them both a copy of the paperwork, then glanced at the empty doorway. Armand also stared out into the hall briefly before asking her to begin.

He's not coming. With a shaky voice, Nicole began to outline the paperwork and the details of the sale. What needed to be signed, what accounts were required for the deposits, things she'd talked about a million times, but this time it felt weird. And wrong.

"I'm sorry I'm late." Destin, looking handsome in a gray suit and tie, whipped into the room and sat next to Elliot. Both Elliot and their father tried to hide their surprise.

Nicole stuttered then and, as if on autopilot, handed him his copy of the packet. Their gazes touched briefly, but he focused quickly on the papers. Nicole saw no emotion in the depths of his eyes.

"We're on page ten," she said to him, annoyed that her

voice sounded low and intimate. He sifted through the papers, the only sound that cut through the icy silence.

"Have you had your vote yet?" Destin asked his father.

"We haven't," Elliot answered.

"Well, I vote yes," said Destin, twirling his pen in his fingers.

The rustling of papers stopped, and Armand cleared his throat. "Destin, I—"

"I said yes, Father." Destin's gaze was challenging.

"Very well," Armand murmured.

They all turned to Nicole, who was pulling her thoughts together.

Why was he doing this? She'd expected him to walk in with some scheme, some reason why they couldn't sell. Instead, he was giving up?

"Okay. Um…so the casino," Nicole started, tapping her pen on the table. "They have the inspection paperwork, but they'll want any permits that have already been secured for the underground cellar. Clay will turn half of that land into a parking lot. He intends to build a pirate ship, if you can believe it. And then there was that lawsuit in New Jersey, something about their construction endangering the water supply. Oh, and he accidentally bulldozed through an animal conservation area in Australia. But I'm sure he'll be more careful here."

The three of them looked at her like she was crazy. And maybe she was. Because she didn't want this deal to go through anymore.

Destin put his papers down and rose from his seat. *Please*, she thought. *Please don't let this go through.*

"I think you all can take it from here. Elliot has the authority to sign any papers for me by proxy. *Au revoir.*"

Destin was gone as swiftly as he'd entered. Nicole stared at the doorway, finding his indifference physically painful. She hung her head, holding back tears, torn between sitting still and running after him. She'd flown across the world and found love; she wasn't going to let him get away that easily.

"Excuse me," Nicole whispered as she stood, unable to meet the eyes of her audience.

Destin was already down the hall when she called out. He slowed, letting her catch up to him, but he didn't stop walking.

"So, that's it?"

"That's it." He was the picture of detachment, and yet his ticking jaw and clenched fists gave him away. He wasn't as unaffected by her as he'd like to let on. She jumped in front of him, making him stop short just inches from her. She could smell his cologne and committed it to memory.

"There's still time. The paperwork needs amendments. No money has been exchanged. Call your friends. Get them down here. Make your father see—"

"Nicole, stop. It's over. It's not my land."

"Yes, it is. You've worked so hard."

"So have you. And I want you to have your sale."

"What?"

"I said, you win." He brought her close and put a hand to her cheek. "I concede. You have a lot more to gain from this than I do. I want you to go back to New York and make the most of it. I'll bet your daughter will be unstoppable, just like her mother."

Their lips touched, and she curled around him for dear life. "I love you," she murmured against his mouth, simultaneously afraid and relieved that she'd let it slip out.

He pulled back slowly, his gaze running over her face. He didn't look happy at her declaration. His steady gaze turned distressed.

He spoke after an excruciatingly long silence. "I wish I knew what to say."

"Well, if you don't know, then there's nothing else," she said with a sad smile.

"No, that's not…what I mean is…" He closed his eyes. "My life is no longer here. I have nothing to offer you. I wish I did. I wish things were different." He studied her face, then lowered his gaze. "Goodbye, Nicole."

And, just like that, he was gone.

It was over.

She'd gotten her sale.

And lost everything.

New York City

Three weeks later, Nicole sat in her new office, going over documents with her two associates. The office contained a mahogany desk, a Persian rug and a leather couch, and there was a huge window with a view of the corner store that was across from Central Park. Not quite the view she had hoped for, but she was big-time now, and that was all that mattered. That had been the goal…right?

Landing in New York had been surreal. She'd told herself it was good to be home and then cried for hours. The tears were a daily occurrence for about two weeks, but she'd gotten good at distracting herself with work, Netflix and wine.

She hadn't heard from Destin, and she hadn't reached out, either. In the back of her mind, a fairy tale played in which he showed up at her office declaring his love. Or, at least, called her on the phone and declared his love. She'd even take something by snail mail if it meant a word from him. If only she could get him out of her head.

Drinks with friends, client lunches, office parties, yoga—the things that had previously given her joy now felt like a burden. Even work no longer gave her that feeling of girl power she'd once had. Being the boss just didn't seem so important anymore.

She typed an email while her two associates gave her an update on a development property in Belize, a place she would have loved to visit, but as a senior director, she no longer had to do the legwork. She took the meetings, vetted the clients, delivered the strategy and put out any fires—without leaving her office. All she had to do now was call the adoption agency.

She didn't know why she hadn't yet.

"And before I forget, Clay Winchester called. Something about Brazil," said Eric, her new assistant.

Nicole stopped typing. Clay was the last person she wanted to talk to. His impulsiveness had cost her the love of her life. No, she couldn't blame it all on Clay. Maybe if she'd told Destin about the offer sooner…her thoughts trailed off.

She still had a vivid picture of how Destin had looked when she'd told him she loved him. Pure fear, with a touch of distress. He'd run like the cops were chasing him. And she just stood there and watched him go. But what had her choices been? He had nothing to give her, he'd said. That included love.

The knock on her door brought her out of her thoughts. Gustavo stood in her doorway, handsome as ever. But her heart no longer fluttered at the sight of him. She'd left it in Brazil.

"May I talk to you?" he asked.

"Of course."

Her team gathered their laptops and hurried out of her office, closing the door behind them. Gustavo took a chair.

"How's it going?"

"Well. It's more paperwork than I thought it would be, but it's good."

"Um, Nicole. I got a call from Clay—you haven't scheduled his team to come in and sign the paperwork yet?"

Nicole struggled to meet his eyes. "I did. Of course I did."

"When is the date?"

"Um…let me check with Eric. He was supposed to send them the draft to review."

"Eric said you told him to hold it."

Nicole swallowed. "Well, something crazy happened. Remember Seguay? He's really into rebuilding the Dechamps winery, maybe even as a silent partner. I just—"

"So you're telling me you purposely put this company at risk by not processing an agreed-upon sale with the Winchester family."

"Well, when you put it that way." She held his gaze for a second. "Yes, I did."

Gustavo's frustrated sigh hurt her more than she thought it would. "Nicole, I need to get that paperwork signed. Right now."

"I can't do that."

Gustavo frowned, his face hardening and his voice rising. "What has gotten into you? I've always supported you, Nicole. This promotion was well deserved, but I can't let you put this company in jeopardy. This deal is closed. You will hand over the original paperwork so we can process this sale!"

Nicole reached into her desk and pulled out a single sheet of paper. "Here's my letter of resignation."

He snatched it from her hand, looking back and forth between her and the letter. "Why?"

"It's a long story. But this sale shouldn't have happened. And I'm trying to make it right." She stood and gathered her purse, taking one more look around the room before meeting her boss's confused gaze. "I don't want you to get hurt in the process, Gustavo. I've learned so much from you. I did this. And I'm sorry."

"I don't understand, Nicole."

"You will. Again, I'm so sorry."

Nicole held her head high and walked briskly from the office, nodding and waving to those she passed in the hallway. She felt guilty, running out like a thief in the night, afraid of what they'd think of her when they found out that she actually did send out the paperwork, just not to Clay.

The original, incomplete copies should be on their way to Porto Alegre and landing on Destin's château doorstep within a day or two. She wasn't even sure he was still living there, but it was the only address she had. If he wasn't, she hoped, somehow, it would be forwarded into his hands.

Then he'd know that the land wasn't gone. His vines were safe, for a little while, at least.

And she wasn't a soulless lawyer who only wanted to make a sale. She was a woman who loved him.

Chapter 21

Rio Grande do Sul...

It wouldn't have worked, Destin told himself over the next couple of weeks. She had a life, a career and a plan. He had—he held up the thick binder of property sale paperwork that had landed on his doorstep two days ago—nothing. She'd said she loved him. At least, she thought she did. Brazil could do that to a person, make them fall in love with love. She'd get over it.

So would he.

That thought stayed with him as he sat in his father's hotel room sipping a glass of wine from their French estate. Exceptional, Nicole had called it. He sighed. When would he stop thinking of her? He could be in the middle of picking brambles from Magnus's coat, and a memory of her would surface—her smiling at the beach, tasting his wine, the way she looked when she kissed him in the night.

He needed those memories to fade. So he could get back to his life, whatever that was.

"I'm glad to see you, Destin," Armand said. Destin noted that his father sat next to him, in the other wooden chair in front of the desk. He'd been avoiding the old man's calls for over a week, but today he had no choice but to see him. "I don't expect you to forgive me."

"And I don't, not yet, anyway. That's not why I'm here." Destin held up the papers and set them on the desk. "This arrived on my doorstep."

Armand took the packet and flipped through the pages, frowning. "It's the sale papers."

"They haven't been processed. A mix-up, I guess. Maybe you should send them to whatshisname."

"Miss Parks sent these to you?"

Destin sucked in a breath at her name. "Like I said, it's probably just a mix-up."

"Have you spoken with her?"

"Why would you ask that?"

"I saw you together, in the hallway during our meeting. The way you looked at her, I thought…"

Destin drained his wine and stood, avoiding his father's eyes. "It's over. And she's gone. Goodbye, Father."

"Destin, wait, please." Armand grabbed two sheets of paper from his desk and handed them to Destin. His father's signature was at the bottom of both.

"What is this?"

"I'm transferring the deed of the property to you." Destin's astonished gaze snapped to his father's. "You were right. Your mother did want you to have it. I've made many mistakes, son, and I don't want this to be one of them. Sign at the bottom, and the land is yours."

"How…when did you do this?" He was afraid to hope, and yet he felt it rising with every breath.

"I decided to call my lawyers after I saw you kissing

Miss Parks in the hallway. This debacle wasn't her fault. It was mine. Then I received a call from Kingsley's saying they'd misplaced the paperwork. I took it as a sign I was doing the right thing. I've already called Mr. Winchester. There will be no sale. I hope you'll accept this land. There are no clauses, no strings attached. You are welcome to have a lawyer review the details. Maybe Miss Parks will review it for you."

"You've spoken to her?"

"No. It seems that Miss Parks no longer works at Kingsley's."

Destin's head whipped up. "What? Where is she?" His father studied his reaction and smiled, sending Destin into a frustrated state. "What are you smiling about?"

"You're in love again, son."

"I'm—" Destin blinked, unable to pull his thoughts together. *Calm, you have to remain calm.* "Where is she?"

"I don't know, but I hope you'll go find her. You deserve to be happy." Destin could only stare at his father. Who was this person? "You know, I met your mother at a conference in London. She had her career there and didn't want to give it up. She was a city girl, I was a country boy. It wasn't easy, but we made it work."

"I never knew she worked in London."

"She had been employed by the *London Times* as a journalist. Quite a demanding job, if I remember. I took the four-hour train to London every weekend just to see her. Those were good times."

The moral of this story wasn't lost on Destin, but a four-hour train ride and a seven-hour plane ride were two very different things. But it wasn't like he couldn't stay for a few weeks at a time. He liked New York.

What was he thinking? She'd told him she loved him, and he'd walked away. If she was smart—and she was—she'd hate him.

Destin looked at the contract, then to his father. He meant it when he said he didn't forgive his father for everything that has happened, but as he stared at the papers, he could already feel his heart lightening.

"What about the debt? What are you going to do?"

"I will figure this out, Destin. I'm a businessman, and no one is going to take my company." Destin had heard that hard edge in his father's voice before. He pitied whoever came up against him.

"Thank you, Father."

"I love you, son." His father's eyes, the ones he saw in the mirror every day, were tearing up.

Destin gripped the papers and swallowed hard. "I love you, as well."

He quit the room before he started to weep. The land was his. *His.* He needed a lawyer. He needed...the elevator was too slow. He raced down the stairs and out into the street.

New York City

"They passed," Nicole said over the phone, doing her best to keep the annoyance from her voice. It was too early in the morning for this.

"For God's sake, why?"

"Honestly, Mr. Dean, everyone I've driven to the estate falls in love with it, until you walk into the living room."

"Then you didn't stage it properly!"

"It's not the staging, it's the smell."

"But the dogs are in a kennel. My precious babies are living in a doggie jail right now because you said it would obstruct the sale to leave them there."

"They are in a dog hotel being treated like royalty. The smell, however, is still lingering. No one is going to spend one point three million dollars on a country home that smells like a pack of wolves."

"They are Japanese Akitas! And all you have to do is burn some candles!"

She imagined it would take a thousand vanilla-coconut pillars just to mask the odor. Then she imagined the place in flames. "I've called another cleaning crew. They'll be there tomorrow."

"I expected more from you, Miss Parks. You're supposed to be the best."

She was the best at international sales, not babysitting dogs or selling smelly celebrity homes. "Mmm-hmm. Sorry you're disappointed. I'm happy to connect you with another agent."

"No! You told me you could sell this. So sell it!"

The phone went dead. And to think she'd thought he was so hot in his last movie. She slumped over her desk and rested her head in her hands. Was it lunchtime yet? She looked at the clock. Nine-thirty in the morning. When had she become a clock-watcher?

When she came back from Brazil. No, she refused to think about him.

She craved another coffee and made her way to the kitchen. From her vantage point, she could see a group of well-dressed men waiting in the lobby. One was flirting with Beverly, the receptionist. Nicole shook her head. Men.

Her new boss appeared, shook their hands and led them back toward the conference rooms.

Tapping her fingers on the granite counter, she waited for the Keurig to fill her coffee, then held the mug in both hands, taking stock of the warmth. She needed it. Nicole wandered into reception.

"Who was that?" she asked Beverly.

"Someone looking for property in France."

Nicole's eyebrows went up, but her interest stalled when she remembered that she no longer worked in international sales. She sighed and sipped her coffee on the way back to her office, wondering if she could actually find a place that would deliver a thousand vanilla candles.

She entered her office and was halfway into her seat when she realized a man in a suit was standing by the back wall gazing up at her Harvard degree plaque.

"Oh, excuse me? Are you looking for the conference room?"

He turned. "No, I'm looking for you."

Her heart stopped.

Destin's dark hair was freshly trimmed, well above the collar of his tailored shirt. His clean-shaven jaw was square and strong, and revealed a small dimple right in the middle of his chin. He was wearing that cologne, the one that made her think of forests and rain.

Nicole had always thought he was handsome with the beard and the cargo pants, but this…damn.

The only thing that kept her from running across the room and strangling him was the supplicating look in his blue eyes.

"Hi, Nicole. How have you been?"

She restrained the urge to burst into an angry rant. Or bitter tears. Actually, she couldn't move. Her pulse was hammering, and the liquid inside her coffee mug was threatening to spill.

"I'm well. You look…" she exhaled "…different."

"You look beautiful. It's so good to see you."

"Is it?" Sarcasm dripped from her tone.

His mouth formed a straight line. "Nicole, I have so much to apologize for. So much to tell you." His palms came up, and he began to step forward, but he halted when she held up her hand.

Setting her quivering coffee on the coaster, she moved

to the side of her desk and perched on the edge, crossing her arms over her chest. "Tell me what?"

"That I'm sorry. I should have answered your calls, your texts. I was blaming you for something that wasn't your fault. I was blaming everyone but myself."

"You could have called to tell me that."

He didn't rise to her snark, just looked around the room, then his gaze came back to hers. "I got your packet. Is that why you left Kingsley's?"

"I didn't want my boss to suffer any consequences of my actions."

He paused. "I owe you, Nicole. I know that must have been hard. Your promotion was on the line." He slowly stepped toward her, as if afraid she'd run off. "I gave the documents to my father. We finally talked. He signed over the land to me. It's mine."

That news made her soul sing, but she kept her cool. "That's good news. What are you going to do?"

"Rebuild. I raised enough to start from scratch. I just need the right people beside me." He was watching her carefully.

She couldn't breathe. "Does that mean I get two cases of free wine?"

"You could have a lifetime of free wine if you wanted it." The deep baritone of his voice triggered a tingling over her skin.

Nicole ground her teeth as she studied him. How many nights had she dreamed of that face, that body? He came closer, so close she could have reached out and touched him if she wanted. And she wanted to…badly.

"Are you happy here?" he asked.

"Yes."

His blue gaze pinned her.

"I don't know. No." She swallowed, unable to look away. "I haven't been happy since you left me at the hotel."

Destin closed in on her, his lips inches from hers, his hands warm as they traveled up and down her back. "Every day, I thought about seeing you again. Doing that day over." A lone tear fell down Nicole's cheek, then another and another. Destin swiped at the tears with his thumb and held her face in his hand. "Don't cry." He kissed her, softly at first and then with more pressure.

Lost in the kiss, she ran her palms up his chest. She trembled from the intensity of his gaze, but she needed more than a nice suit and a shave to get past the hurt of him walking away. She jerked back and wriggled from his grasp.

"I appreciate your apology, but you don't get to just waltz in here and act like everything is okay."

"I shouldn't have left you like that. I'd take it back if I could. I'd take back a lot of mistakes I made. I wasted so much time, but then, if I hadn't, I never would have met you. You're the only thing I don't regret."

Stunned by the sincerity in his face, she murmured, "Why did you come?"

He straightened his tie and grinned. "I need a lawyer."

Her eyes narrowed. It wasn't the declaration she was looking for, and he knew it. She shook her head and stuck out her hip. "I don't know whether to slap you or kiss you."

"I'll take the latter." With one quick jerk, she was in his arms, crushed against him, their mouths locked and molded perfectly. He broke the kiss only for a moment. "I love you, Nicole. I'm sorry I didn't say it sooner."

Someone behind them cleared their throat, and they turned to see her new boss standing in the doorway. Nicole stiffened; she needed to keep this job.

"Mr. Dechamps," the older man began to stutter with a frown. "Uh, we've been looking for you. We're ready to start when you are. I didn't know you, uh, knew Nicole." His eyes slid to her.

"We're ready," Destin said. Then he turned to Nicole. "Right?"

"We are?"

Destin turned to her. "Seguay's legal team is here. My father is selling a portion of his land in France to him for a wellness resort."

"You're kidding. But won't that hurt his wine output?"

"Father is letting me streamline his production. I'm going to make him more efficient."

She smiled. "I'm so proud of you. You came to help your father."

His gaze turned serious. "No, Nicole, I came here for you."

Destin turned to Nicole's boss, still in the doorway. "Miss Parks will be joining us."

"Sir, Miss Parks doesn't handle our international territory."

"I know. But she handles mine."

Nicole held back a smile when her boss began muttering under his breath. She grabbed her papers and followed Destin out of her office, stopping to give a folder to the scowling man. "Richard Dean," she said gravely. "Actor. He has nine dogs." She dropped the files into her boss's hands, chuckling when she glimpsed his face.

She caught up to Destin before he entered the conference room and pulled him to the side. "Hey, one more thing before we go in there. I love you, too."

She kissed him quickly, then skirted around him to join the group.

Epilogue

Rio Grande do Sul, eighteen months later

Nicole hurried into the kitchen of the main house just as Luiza was placing the tops of toasted French buns on two fully stacked roast beef sandwiches. Nicole had been so busy that morning planning for the incoming guests that she'd skipped breakfast. Her stomach rumbled as Luiza's staff prepared the daily menu, and the savory smells permeated the fully modernized kitchen—stainless steel appliances, granite countertops, track lighting and a wood-burning oven.

Just steps away was a fully stocked bar with seating, a couch-lined lounge area by a stone fireplace and a large room of rustic dining tables. A glass wall overlooked the landscaped courtyard, and the picturesque countryside boasted rows upon rows of healthy grape vines.

They'd done it. Vin Amante Winery and Resort was alive. Twice a day, tour buses dropped off locals and foreigners seeking the wine and relaxation that *Travel and Leisure* magazine had rated five out of five stars. Their second wave of guests should be arriving at any moment for an afternoon of wine tasting along with a four-course lunch.

She smiled to herself when she saw the giant pot of rabbit stew simmering on the stove.

"Is he still down there?" Nicole asked Luiza in Portuguese, the language coming more naturally now.

"*Sim*, we haven't seen him all morning." Luiza placed their plates on a silver tray and slid it in front of Nicole.

"This Bauru looks amazing." Nicole plucked a few french fries from Destin's plate and popped them into her mouth. With a knowing smile, Luiza tossed a few more fries on the plate.

"Ooooh, can I get a little cup of the stew, too?" Nicole added, and Luiza complied.

Nicole marched the tray across the lawn toward the cellar. Through the trees, she studied the spa facility that was just a short walk from the winery's main house. Standing outside on the steps, Anton was overseeing the departure of their resort guests. The few guests she could see had smiles on their faces. She nodded, knowing firsthand the healing powers of the outdoor bathhouse, massage rooms, yoga gazebo and sauna.

Reaching the cellar, Nicole flung the door open, and her heels echoed on the stairs. It was still an unassuming gray structure on the outside, but the inside, through the doors and down the stairs, had been transformed into a comfortable space. There were electric sconces on the walls and a large chandelier hung majestically over the refurbished dining table—which was raised to accommodate twelve high-backed chairs. Their greatest addition was the luxury bedroom with the king-sized bed they'd added in the back alcove.

It didn't compare to their bedroom at the château, but it came in handy when they worked late.

Bottles upon bottles of Dechamps label and Vin Amante label wines lined the walls, but only a few were out and ready for the tasting tours.

Magnus met her at the last step, and she slipped him some fries from Destin's plate. Then she grabbed a Vin Amante bottle from the shelf and set it on the table next to their food.

"Destin, it's lunchtime!" she called out toward the bedroom. "I have to scarf this down before the buses get here."

Nicole found a bottle opener on the island in their stocked kitchenette, but paused when she spied a row of glasses with mini pours of red wine. She peeked around to the lounge area and found the leather couch empty, but the electric fireplace was still on. She raised an eyebrow when she realized the bedroom door was closed.

"Baby," she said, moving toward the door. "Are you asleep?"

Just as she reached for the knob, Destin opened the door, stepped through, and closed it behind him.

He blinked and cleared his throat. "Hey."

"Hey." She blinked back. His hair looked like he'd been running his hand through it. *Can this man ever not look sexy?* She noticed he was wearing the green plaid button-down she'd bought him in New York.

"What are you doing?" she asked.

"Nothing." He smiled and pulled her against him, softly claiming her lips. She had more questions, but she forgot them when he deepened their kiss. Her arms linked around his neck, and her fingers teased his nape.

"Let's go in the bedroom," she whispered against his mouth.

She felt him pause and frowned.

"I need you over here first."

Destin led her to sit at the dining table and brought over the wine glasses from the kitchenette. He slid the first one in front of her. "Taste."

He was a maniac. He'd begun thinking up new formulas the minute the renovations were done. She loved his obsession, though, because it made him happy. His gaze was so intense today, she wondered what was so special about these three infusions. She gave the glass a swish, held it to her nose and then tipped it into her mouth. She let it sit on her tongue and frowned dramatically; she knew he was dying to stump her.

"This is your father's Cabernet Franc. Is this the two-year-old batch?"

He huffed. "How do you do it?"

She shrugged. "What have you been doing down here all morning?"

Another wine glass appeared in front of her. Destin bent to her ear and kissed it before whispering, "You'll never guess this one." She turned over her shoulder to capture his lips, but he quickly stepped to the side. He was up to something, and it spurred her on to beat him at his own game.

Lifting her gaze to his, she slowly licked her lips, then ran her tongue along the edge of the glass before taking a sip. His lips parted, and she ran her gaze down his body before returning her attention to the glass in her hand.

"This is Vin Amante. Maybe a year old. It's developing nicely."

Destin pressed his lips together and shoved the third glass on the table. With a triumphant smile, she grabbed the glass and tossed the garnet liquid back without her usual ritual…and stilled.

Clove, chocolate, elderflower, oak, truffle. Her brows drew together. "What is this?"

"Do you like it?"

"It's a Cab Franc. Spicy, but subtle. I like it a lot."

"Like you." He placed a mock-up of a violet wine label in front of her. Her name was written in gold in the center. "I began tinkering with the flavors the week we met."

Tears formed quickly in her eyes. She rose and pulled him close, kissing his lips through the wet tracks over her mouth. She knew how much the wine meant to him, and it was a true declaration of his love to include her.

"Thank you. It's a beautiful gift."

"You're welcome, but that's not all." He led her to the bedroom and opened the door.

The dimly lit chandelier covered the bed in a warm glow and placed a spotlight on the small velvet box sitting open on the red duvet. Nicole's heart raced as she stepped forward, her gaze fixed on the ring's huge princess-cut diamond. She blew out the breath she was involuntarily holding and let the tears again fall from her eyes.

Destin's arms surrounded her. He kissed her neck and the side of her face, then whispered against her cheek.

"Marry me."

Like she'd refuse. She'd fallen for him the day they met, literally. Breaking his grasp, she reached for the ring and slipped it on her finger, noticing the halo of small diamonds in the setting and around the band. It fit perfectly. Then she turned to him and began unbuttoning her blouse.

"I will, on one condition."

His gaze got caught on her open blouse. "Anything."

"I want a family," she breathed, letting her skirt fall to the floor.

He blinked and swallowed hard. She smiled at the surprise in his eyes. "She'll have your eyes, but my brains," Nicole said, tossing her shirt on the floor.

A slow smile spread across his face and he walked toward her, pulling his own shirt over his head. "He'll have your smile, but my spirit."

"She'll be stubborn," she said playfully, sliding onto the bed in her lingerie.

"He'll be level-headed," he teased, following her and covering her body with his own.

Later, lying in each other's arms, hot and sweaty in the rumpled covers, their hearts full, they smiled at each other in between tiny kisses.

"I think you've gotten over your aversion to lawyers," Nicole said, gazing at Destin from the crook of his arm. Her ring sparkled where her hand rested against his chest.

Destin rolled toward her and pressed the length of her body against his. Breathing hard, he pulled her closer with a satisfied smile. "Only one lawyer." He kissed her, then pulled back quickly, his brows drawn. "Do you miss New York?"

Nicole twisted her lips. She missed her friends, but she was able to fly them to the resort for free. Her girls had already visited three times and had plans to come in another month. And Nicole occasionally did business in New York for Seguay—he'd decided that if any city needed healing, it was NYC.

"No, not really."

"What about negotiating a hard sell or closing a deal? You used to love that."

Nicole held up her ring. "Well, we've just entered into a partnership," she said, pushing him onto his back and straddling his hips. "So if you'd like to start negotiations now, I'm ready."

Nicole smiled against Destin's lips, content, her blood still pumping after closing the most significant deal of her life.

* * * * *